# The

# Ride

## BY

## JUSTIN REICHMAN

Scobre Press Corporation
2255 Calle Clara
La Jolla, CA 92037

Scobre Press books may be purchased for educa-
tional, business or sales promotional use.

Edited by Helen Glenn Court
Illustrated by Gail Piazza
Cover Design by Michael Lynch

ISBN 1-933423-26-9

TOUCHDOWN EDITION

www.scobre.com

# CHAPTER ONE

# BIG CHILL

I was in the gate with less than a minute remaining before the last heat of the day. I guess I should have been nervous, but I wasn't. I was more excited than anything. Standing at the top of the Big Chill—the hardest and best run on Rockville Mountain—I knew that there was no room for mistakes. If I ate it on this mountain, I was going to eat it bad. More people got injured on the Big Chill than any other run in Wyoming. I think that most of them get hurt because they don't know the run. I've ridden it so many times I could probably do it with my eyes closed. Not that I would ever snowboard with my eyes closed.

"Thirty seconds," the race official manning the gate called out.

I quickly double checked my binding, making sure it was nice and tight. Then I pulled my goggles over my helmet, trying not to get them caught in my long brown hair. I was ready. I was psyched.

"Ten seconds."

I began to rock my board back and forth in the gate. It glided easily across the snow. I compared myself to a jockey sitting on a horse just before a race. I took one final, excited, deep breath. Then I blew out, hard, puffing my cheeks.

"Five, four, three, two, one . . . Go!" The gun sounded.

I flew out of the gate the instant it opened. The first part of the run was an almost vertical narrow chute. So I crouched down low to provide as little wind resistance as possible. I couldn't turn this early in the race. All I could do was tuck, pick up speed, and not fall down. After a few seconds, the slope became a bit less steep. Although I was moving at a good clip, I had a second to look around and get my bearings. There wasn't much to see: the trees and rocks were a total blur. I smiled from ear to ear.

The narrow chute that begins the run opens into a small bowl about a hundred yards down the mountain. We had gotten some fresh powder the night before, so my board sunk down when it first touched the snow. I leaned back to distribute my weight, and with luck glide more easily over the fresh stuff. The snow sprayed behind me, and a thin mist of powder hit my face. At that moment, it felt as if I were flying. I knew I was winning and it was perfect.

I wanted to turn and enjoy the fresh new pow-pow, but there was no time for that. I was racing—racing the clock. In the last heat of the day, I was so far ahead of the other racers that it would have taken a really big screw-up to blow my lead. But I wanted to win big. So I fought through the powder, turning only when I absolutely had to. Otherwise, I kept my line straight down the bowl. I was really cooking. Not out of control, though. I'm never out of control—especially on the Big Chill.

The powder bowl opened into a groomed mogul field. A

mogul is a big hard mound of snow on a run. It's not a jump—it's more of an obstacle. If you hit a mogul the wrong way, you'll face plant. If you face plant when you're going as fast as I go, it hurts, even when you're wearing a helmet. I knew every bump on the run, though. There was no way I would hit one wrong.

Sure enough, I navigated through the mogul field with precision. My knees were shock absorbers. My board was an extension of my legs. I got a little bit of air a couple of times, but nothing too big. This was all about speed. I took each bump exactly as planned, and when I landed, I was ready for the next one.

After I passed through the mogul field, there was a final jump before the finish line. It wasn't much. But when you're going fast, even a little jump can turn into big air. I tucked down low and really went for it. I wanted this to be the best run of the day. Not just my best run, but *the* best run. Period.

My board lifted off the ground and I was literally flying. I grabbed the rails with both hands. I could see the finish in front of me. There was a small crowd that had gathered. I tried not to look at them, avoiding anything that might throw off my concentration. From the corner of my eye, though, something seemed out of the ordinary. I turned my head ever so slightly to the left, and wondered: is that a gorilla wearing a clown wig?

Just like that, it was over. I lost control for a second—a split second. My balance shifted. Not too much, but just enough to screw up my landing. The first thing to hit the snow was the front edge of my board. I was moving forward at full speed, so when I hit the ground, I hit hard. My board dug deep in the snow and stopped when it hit the frozen surface. Of course, my body flew forward, the momentum continuing to move me at an insane speed.

I hit the packed snow about ten feet in front of where my board landed. I hit hard, with a loud thud that I could hear and feel in my ears. Instantly, the breath was knocked from my lungs. My teeth rattled inside my head.

This was simply not supposed to be happening to me, especially not on the Big Chill. This was supposed to be my run!

Everything became a blur after that. My mouth and nose filled with snow. My goggles flew off my helmet. I opened and closed my eyes as I flipped and spun and rolled down the hill. I caught a glimpse of the sky, then snow, then clouds, then more snow. I kept flipping. I tried to stop, but there was nothing I could do. I was moving too fast to take a spill like that.

I ended up flat on my back, sliding down the hill. When I opened my eyes, I saw that I had rolled past the finish line. I leaned up and looked at the crowd staring down at me on the ground. Sure enough, mixed in the middle of a large group of people was some idiot wearing a gorilla suit and a clown wig. What was that guy thinking? Moron. Was he trying to get someone killed?

I squinted to get a closer look at the bib the person was wearing on his gorilla chest. It read, "I go ape for Mad Marty in the Mornings on 104.5." As I finished reading those words, I realized exactly who the idiot in the gorilla suit was. My father—Mad Marty Morgan.

There might have been a time in my life when I was more furious with my dad, but at that moment I couldn't remember it. I sat up, stretching my body to make sure I hadn't broken any bones. Then I got to my feet, feeling all right physically. That was when I began planning how I was going to move out of my house and into my best friend Sally's—far, far, away from my embarrassing, gorilla-suit-wearing father.

Just then, a voice came over the loudspeakers, "despite her unconventional finish, Cece Morgan nabs first place in the thirteen-and-under girls' category." This announcement was followed by some applause from the crowd. I gave a wave. "And with the last heat of the day," the voice went on, "we have the final results. The overall winner of the Rockville Junior Snowboard Jam is. . ." I took a deep breath. ". . . Chad Doogan." I let out a big sigh.

My name is Cece Morgan, not Chad Doogan. I know Chad Doogan, and he's a jerk. I undid my binding and walked away from the crowd. I wanted to go home. At least I wasn't injured from my big wipeout, which I guess was lucky. At the moment, though, I didn't feel very lucky. I thought I might just be the unluckiest person on the planet. How many other kids had a gorilla for a father?

I walked over to the tent where they served hot chocolate and posted the day's results. It was in black and white, clear as day. Chad Doogan, the biggest jerk in all of Rockville, had beaten me by 3.2 seconds. 3.2 seconds! Guess how many seconds slower my last heat was from the one before it? Four seconds.

That wipeout cost me the championship. I felt like punching something. I felt like crying. I felt like screaming at the top of my lungs. I felt a tap on my shoulder. I turned around. There was no one there. I felt a tap on my other shoulder. I turned around again. There was still no one there. I only knew one person who was childish enough to think this was funny. I stared straight ahead and hissed through my teeth, "Stop it, Dad."

"Congratulations, Chili," said my father, with a muffled voice—muffled because of the mask he was wearing. I ignored him. I crossed my arms tight across my chest. "Come on, Chili, you won your age group. That's fantastic!"

He didn't get it. Winning my age group wasn't enough. Today was supposed to be my day! I was *supposed* to win the whole thing! The reason I didn't win was because of him. He just didn't get it.

I finally turned around. It was worse than I imagined. Not only was my dad a gorilla, he was also a clown. He was wearing a full gorilla suit, complete with big bushy brown body hair and a dark mask. On top of his mask sat a big rainbow-colored clown wig. He wore ridiculously large mirrored sunglasses as well. My angry reflection stared back at me from his shades. A big red clown nose hung from his face. From the slopes, I hadn't realized that he was also wearing matching rainbow suspenders and a yellow bow tie. And, oh yeah, a giant diaper.

This was my father. "Dad, please walk away from me. Pretend we don't know each other."

"What's wrong, Chili?" he asked, pulling his mask off. His light brown and gray hair stuck straight up from the static electricity. He looked at me with concern through his light hazel eyes. The same eyes I had.

"Dad, I never would have wiped out like that if you weren't wearing that stupid costume. You made me blow my concentration! And if I didn't crash, I would have won. I would have beaten Chad Doogan."

My dad stared at me, silent for a moment. "Beaten Doogan, huh?"

I nodded.

"Chili, I'm sorry." He hung his head, "I just came to see

you race. You know I would never do anything to screw up your racing. Today is such a crowded day, I thought I'd advertise for the show—you know." He stared down at the snow again, then back up at me. "Honey, you were great out there! This whole place was going bananas for you."

"Bananas, dad?" I started to smile at him in his gorilla suit, but I stopped myself.

"It's true. They were going absolutely ape!" he smiled at me again. "I'm sorry."

When Dad looked at me like that, it was almost impossible to stay mad at him. So instead, I just smiled. "Let's go, Dad. You are such a goofball." I grabbed his arm and we made our way toward the parking lot. I knew he didn't mean to blow my concentration. He really is a great person. He's just kind of weird.

Just before we made a clean getaway into the parking lot, Chad Doogan walked up to me. "Great race, Cece. I was worried there for a second. It really came down to the wire. Lucky for me that jump got you at the end. Now *that's* drama." He smiled his insincere cocky smile. I wanted to tackle him. "Better luck next year," he said. He turned to face my dad. "Hey, Mr. Morgan. Love the outfit." He laughed and walked away.

I was quiet for most of the ride home. I could have been a winner.

# CHAPTER TWO

## GROWING UP CHILI

My name is Cece, but my dad calls me Chili. I'm not exactly sure why, but he's called me that since I was five years old. I'm twelve now and I'm in sixth grade. I guess I'm about average height, with an athletic build and long brown hair. People say I have a pretty face. But people used to think the world was flat, too, and you know how that theory turned out.

Anyway, my whole life I've lived in Rockville, Wyoming—population 6,537. I've read enough books and watched enough television to know that I live in a very small town. Downtown Rockville is just a single block long. There's Pick 'n Save Grocery store, two banks, Rockville Public Library, Wendell's Drug Store, Rockville Hardware, Rockville Post Office, Clean-as-a-Whistle Dry Cleaners, Tony and Terry's Pizza and Pasta, Jon's Big Burger, and Captain Good Licks, which has the best ice cream on the planet. That's it and that's all. If you need some clothes or want to see a movie, you have to go to Jackson Hole, which is about a thirty-minute drive when it's not snowing.

If you were from out of town and you drove through Rockville, you would probably think there wasn't anything to do. You'd probably think that the people who lived here were dying of boredom. But you would be wrong, because there is one thing we have here that is pretty much bigger and better than anywhere else. We have the best, most beautiful mountain to snowboard on—which, by the way, is my favorite thing in the world to do. *Snowboarding Times* called Rockville Mountain one of the best-kept secrets in the USA. When that article came out, I remembered hoping that nobody outside of Rockville read it. The last thing we need is lots of tourists clogging up our mountain.

I can be up on the mountain, linking my first turns on the best-kept secret snow in the country fourteen minutes from my front door. There's enough snow to snowboard from October to April. So, for six months of the year, I am as far from being bored as Rockville is from the big city. I snowboard on weekend days and at least three days during the week.

When vacations come around, I don't like to go anywhere, I stay home and snowboard. I'm good at it—and yes—I guess you could say that I am a little obsessed with it. I've been doing it for so long, I can't remember when I didn't know how to do it.

One thing you should know about me is that I only like things I'm good at. My English teacher, Mrs. Cruickshank, thinks this is a big problem. She only thinks so because I'm not very good at English, so I hate it. For some reason, she is simply positive that I'm better than a C student in English. She's constantly saying stuff like, "If you tried half as hard in English as you do with your snowboarding, you'd be doing just fine, Cece." She might be right, too.

This past year, we've been working a lot on finding themes in the books we're reading. I haven't found any yet. I sometimes feel like taking my book and throwing it through the window I sit next to. Instead, I pretend I am snowboarding and space out. Which I think is okay, because daydreaming and *not* finding themes is a whole lot better than a broken window. Only Mrs. Cruickshank doesn't seem to think so.

If you ask my science teacher, Mr. Low, about me, he'll tell you that I'm applying myself just fine—better than fine, in fact. You see, I love science. I love learning how everything around us and inside us works. I'm the top student in his class, probably the school, maybe the district, could be the state. I got an A-plus last semester, and when Mr. Low gave us our grades he told me that I was going to be a great doctor someday.

I'm not sure if I want to be a doctor when I grow up, but I do know that I want to do something serious and important, unlike my dad. My dad's real name is Martin Chadwick Morgan. To everyone in Rockville, though, and most of Wyoming, he's Mad Marty in the Morning. Dad hosts the Mad Marty Morning radio show on 104.5 FM. He describes his show as "a warm cup of wacky wake up on your way to work."

Being Mad Marty makes my dad do a lot of un-Dad-like things, like wearing a clown-gorilla costume with a giant diaper. His show is the number one morning radio show in Wyoming. Most kids at school think I'm lucky. They think having a semi-celebrity dad would make me proud. To be honest, I love my dad and I am proud of him—but a lot of times he really embarrasses me.

Dads aren't supposed to spend weekend afternoons in the

garage inventing new radio contests involving super bouncy balls. They aren't supposed to scuba dive in giant pools full of chocolate pudding. And they definitely aren't supposed to compete in hot dog eating contests while wearing t-shirts with pictures of heavy metal bands on them.

Dads are supposed to be more like my mom—responsible and serious. My mom is vice president of Snow Leopard Gear, which is the fourth-largest manufacturer of outdoor clothing in the world. She's not a local celebrity like my dad, but she works hard and is very important in the company. It's pretty cool for me because I get all the free jackets, pants, shirts, gloves, hats, goggles, socks, and long underwear I could ever want. And Snow Leopard Gear is really good stuff.

It's not totally perfect having such a responsible and serious mom either. There's a lot to do when you're vice president of a huge company. Sure, she keeps away from gorilla suits, and hardly ever embarrasses me. That's mostly because I barely see her. Mom works all the time. Plus, she goes on lots of business trips to places like China and Switzerland. Sometimes she'll be gone for two or three weeks at a time. Once she went to Iceland and was gone for two months, leaving me alone with my dad.

When she's not traveling, she might as well be gone anyway. She's in the office every day, even on most weekends. And most nights, I go to bed before she comes home. My mom started working at Snow Leopard designing jackets and worked her way up to the top. She's very determined and driven. I really admire her, but most of the time I miss her.

So those are my parents. Although my life definitely isn't perfect, I'm a pretty happy person. I *do* have two of the best friends a person could ever ask for. One is Sally Peterson. The other is Oscar the Wonder Poodle. Sally and I have been friends since we were in diapers. Sally and I do everything together, except snowboard. Sally's not really an outdoors type of person. We watch a lot of movies, shop in Jackson Hole, talk on the phone, and eat lunch together every day. On the weekends, I'm either spending the night at Sally's or she's spending the night at my house. Even though she doesn't like being outside in the cold, she comes to most of my competitions to cheer me on. That's how good a friend she is.

And then there's Oscar. Oscar is a standard poodle, but there's nothing standard about him. He doesn't have one of those disgusting poofy haircuts like those poodles on the dog shows on the Animal Planet. Oscar is rugged and loves being outside. He loves going on walks, playing in the snow, and when you talk to him, he cocks his head and stares at you. Oscar's the best dog in the world. He understands everything I say to him.

# CHAPTER THREE

## THE PHONE CALL

The phone rang at 7:34 in the morning. I knew it wasn't for me, because Sally's the only person who ever calls me—and she was asleep in the bed on the other side of the room. The loud ringing woke me, along with Sally and Oscar. We had been up late the night before, watching movies and talking—except for Oscar, who just watched movies and listened. A phone call at 7:34 on a Sunday morning was not my top choice of ways to start the day.

My parents get lots of phone calls for work. I could tell this one was for my dad from the bits and pieces of the conversation I could pick up from the heating vent in my room: "Yes, hello . . . no it's fine . . . uh huh, uh huh . . . huh? You're joking!" My dad's voice got louder. "You're kidding! Leave Wyoming? Well, I never thought about it. They want us when? Next week! Uh, huh . . . uh huh . . . Well, that sounds great! Thank you so much. Los Angeles, here we come!"

I shot up from the bed, fully awake. I looked at Oscar, then

Sally. I couldn't believe what I had just heard. Did Sally hear it too?

"Did my dad just say Los Angeles here we come?"

"I don't think so," said Sally, yawing. She seemed half asleep still.

"I'm sure that's what he said. We're moving to Los Angeles next week." I started to panic. "I can't move to Los Angeles. There are too many people in Los Angeles. There's no snowboarding in Los Angeles. You are too far away from Los Angeles. I cannot move to Los Angeles."

"Calm down, Cece. You are not moving anywhere." Sally sat up and stretched her arms. "Remember when you were convinced you got the black lung disease when we took the field trip to the Museum of Mining, but it turned out to be just the dust that was making you sneeze? This is probably the same thing. You're not moving to Los Angeles," she laughed, as if it was no big deal.

This calmed me down quite a bit. After all, Sally had a good point. I do tend to overreact. She was always able to get me to relax. "Maybe you're right. But I swear that's what I heard." I threw my covers off and got out of bed. "Before I officially start freaking, I'll go check it out. It's probably nothing." I opened my door and whispered, "I'll be right back."

I stepped quietly into the hallway. As I approached my parents' door, I could hear their voices. They were fighting. It was a noise that I had gotten pretty used to. Their voices were always hushed when they fought. Lately, they fought pretty much whenever they were together—which was hardly ever, because Mom worked so much. They tried to hide their fighting from me, but that was pointless. I could hear them through the vent in my room. Besides, I could always tell when they had been arguing anyway. After a fight, my dad would be extra-special nice to me, and my mom would get really, really quiet. Sometimes she would even leave the house for a few hours. Same thing every time.

Carefully, I put my ear up to their door. I could hear everything: "What am I supposed to do, just pack up and leave my job?" my mom asked.

"This is the opportunity of a lifetime."

"This is the opportunity of *your* lifetime."

"This is good for all of us."

"How is moving to the worst city in America good for all of us?"

"I don't think that's fair."

"No, what I don't think is fair is uprooting your family for the sole purpose of your betterment. What am I going to do in Los Angeles? I can't just ask the company to move over there. I've worked eleven years to get where I am. Am I just supposed to walk away from it?"

"Can't you even be the least bit happy for me? This is a dream come true."

"Have you thought about your daughter? Can you imagine how she's going to handle this? Los Angeles, Martin?"

This was not good. For the first time in my life, I was right, not over-reacting. I stood frozen outside my parents' bedroom. I simply couldn't move.

I heard my mom say. "I have to get out of here for a while." Suddenly the door flung open. My mom was surprised to see me standing there. "Oh, Cece," she said.

I stood quiet for a second. "The phone woke me up."

"So I guess you heard then?" She winced a little bit. "You

heard everything?"

I nodded.

My dad appeared behind her with a serious look on his face. "Well, I guess we should all talk about this." This was one of the first times I could remember him not making a joke out of a situation. I knew right then, that this was for real.

A few minutes later, Mom and I drove Sally home. I don't think Sally really understood what was happening, because she actually seemed excited about the whole situation. We both sat in the back seat. "Do you think you're going to live next door to a movie star? I wonder who it's gonna be."

"Not now, Sally."

"I just can't believe this. I can't wait to visit. I've been waiting my whole life to get out of this town, and now you're really doing it, Cece! Los Angeles!" My mom shot Sally a look that shut her up for the rest of the ride.

When Mom and I got back home, we sat down at the kitchen table with my dad. I couldn't remember the last time we had all been together like this. At first, everyone just stared at something silently. Dad looked at Mom. She stared out the window. I focused on the kitchen table—I hated that kitchen table. The tiles were all different shapes, sizes, and colors and it was really ugly. Mom bought it at some fancy art auction years ago. It's supposed to be some great piece of art, but I think it's hideous. Having this conversation was hard enough—doing it while sitting at that table, though, was downright impossible.

"I'm sorry you heard all of that," my dad said, looking over at me.

Mom nodded.

Dad kept talking. "I guess it's good in a way that we all found out about this at the same time. That way we can decide about this as a family."

I stared at the disgusting table.

"Meaning your father can convince us all to move to Los Angeles for him," my mother remarked.

"Let's try to be constructive here," my father countered.

"I just don't see how this is going to be a *conversation* when it's clear that you are going to move no matter what."

"That's not true."

I kept looking at the table. The tiles seemed to be spinning and dancing in circles as they argued. I really didn't want to be part of this.

"Oh, really? You're going to call up the studio and say, 'My wife and daughter don't want to leave Rockville so thanks for the offer, but I think I'm going to pass on it.' That's what could come out of this discussion?" Mom stared out the window and shook her head.

I was lost in the tiles.

Mom stood up. "I don't think we're going to get anywhere. Cece, I'm sorry you're in the middle of this. I'm going for a walk." With that, she left the house. She didn't quite slam the door, but did close it forcefully behind her. It was just me and my dad and the kitchen table.

We sat in silence for a moment. "So, Chili, what do you think about all this?"

"Huh?" I knew this was supposed to be a really important discussion we were having, but I couldn't think of anything to say. Too many things were going on in my head. Too much was happening.

"How would you feel about moving to Los Angeles?"

When he put it like that, something in me snapped to attention. "Terrible. Miserable. Horrible. That's how I'd feel." I said this matter-of-factly. Then I jumped up from the table and ran into my room. I slammed the door as hard as I could behind me. Oscar jumped up from my bed, startled. I pet him to calm him down. Then I started crying.

At that moment, I knew I'd be moving to Los Angeles in a week and there was nothing I could say or do about it. Dad's mind was made up. All the begging and screaming in the world wasn't going to change what was about to happen. We were going to move. You'd have better luck stopping an avalanche with a spoon than stopping my dad from taking his dream job in Los Angeles.

For the rest of that night Dad did his best to be nice to me. He tried to tell me over and over again how this was going to be really great and how I should keep an open mind. "There's a reason so many people live in Los Angeles, Cece, it's a great place." I refused to listen to him. He only wanted me to feel excited about moving to Los Angeles so he wouldn't have to feel guilty about destroying my life.

# CHAPTER FOUR

## CECE AND SALLY

"You can stay with me," Sally said. "My parents love you. Or I could go instead of you."

Sally and I were sitting on the swings at Homestead Park. We spent a lot of time there. The park has two swings, a slide, and monkey bars. Because it's so small, nobody really goes there. Except Sally and me. We meet there when we need to talk about important stuff and we don't want anyone to hear us. There's a little patch of grass for Oscar to run around, which he likes. It's our perfect secret meeting place.

We sat in silence for a minute. Then I looked down at Oscar, who was lying down in front of us. "What do you think about all of this, boy?"

He cocked his head the way he did to let me know he understood me.

"He'll have fun in LA," Sally said.

I smiled. "Yeah, I bet he will. I think a big beautiful poodle like him is going to fit in a lot better than I will."

I twisted the chain of the swing around and kicked my feet in the patch of dirt that was worn away under the swing. Looking down at the patch, I noticed how big it was. It seemed too big to be made just by Sally and me. It suddenly occurred to me that other people must have swung on these swings, and maybe even talked about the same kind of stuff that Sally and I talked about. This thought made me feel weird.

"Wait a minute, you can't go." This was the moment it finally hit Sally. I was *really* moving. She was so excited about the big city that she hadn't seriously thought about what moving meant. "You can't break up Cece and Sally. We were supposed to be together forever. You can't leave me alone here." Sally looked down at her feet. "It's going to be awful without you here. This isn't fair."

"I know."

Sally was quiet. She kept staring at her feet, kicking at the dirt. She looked back up at me and tears were streaming down her cheek. "This really stinks."

"Come on, Sally. LA's not that far away. We'll write. There's the phone, e-mail, and you can come visit me in the summer. We'll go to Disneyland, Universal Studios, Hollywood, Beverly Hills. And you never know what famous neighbor I might have." I don't know why, but all of a sudden, I was trying to turn this into a good thing. I guess I couldn't stand to see Sally upset.

"What about snowboarding?" she asked.

That was the magic question. I paused for a while before I spoke. "Well," I finally said, "it will give me a good excuse to come home all the time." We smiled at each other.

When Sally left the park she seemed to be feeling a little

better. I went home and felt worse. Disneyland, Universal Studios, Hollywood, Beverly Hills—these things sounded great, but they just weren't me. I was a snowboarder from Wyoming, not a Californian.

By the time I got to my front door, I was near tears. I couldn't imagine a life without the mountains. I couldn't imagine a life without snowboarding. That's when I decided to check something out. I mean, there had to be *some* snowboarding near Los Angeles. It wasn't like I was moving to the moon.

I went online, and within a few minutes, I found that the closest mountain—Big Bison—was a three-hour drive from my new home. That was pretty far, but at least there was someplace I could go to snowboard. I decided to give them a call.

"Big Bison."

"Yeah, hi. How much snow do you have at your base right now?"

"Uh, I don't know," said the clueless guy on the other end of the line.

"If you had to guess, what would you say?"

He paused for a long time. "Why would I have to guess?"

"Let's say that someone was calling you on the phone, right?'

"Yeah," he answered.

This might have been the stupidest person I had ever spo ken to. "Okay. Let's say this person was curious as to how much snow there was on your mountain because she was a really big snowboarder. What would you tell her?"

"I'd probably put Steve on the phone," he said.

"Okay, can I speak to Steve?" I asked.

"Steve's not working today."

"Well, thanks, bye." I quickly hung up the phone. That was a pretty frustrating conversation. It was looking more and more like snowboarding was out of the picture for good. In less than a week I'd be losing two of my favorite things: snowboarding and Sally. Thanks a lot, Dad.

I didn't see how things could get worse, but somehow they did. Right after I hung up the phone, my parents called me downstairs for another family meeting. I asked them this time if we could sit in the living room. We have a glass coffee table in the living room that's much less offensive than the kitchen table.

My dad began. "Cece, your mother and I have been doing some talking. This show is a dream come true for me. I can't pass up the opportunity. On the other hand, your mother's job right now is her dream. She's worked very hard to get to where she is."

"That's right," my mom cut in.

"And it wouldn't be fair for her to just walk out on what she worked so hard to accomplish."

Mom nodded.

"So we've decided that you and I are going to go out to Los Angeles first—to check things out. It'll be fun. I promise. School will just be starting its spring term, so it will be a good time for you to. . . "

"Mom's not coming?" I asked, looking at my dad. "You're not coming with us?" I turned to her. She stared back at me with tears welling up in her eyes.

Dad continued, "She's going to continue her job here."

"Well, I want to stay too." I said.

Mom chimed in. "It's not that simple, Cece. With your dad in Los Angeles, there would be nobody here to look after you. My work schedule is just too crazy."

"I can look after myself."

"This is the only way it's going to work, Chili. Mom will start looking for work in Los Angeles. When she finds something as good as what she has here in Rockville, she'll come join us."

She's never going to move to Los Angeles, I thought. I'm never going to see my mother again.

"I know it will be hard for a while, Cece," Mom said, "but this is the best we can do right now."

I didn't see how splitting up the family would be best. I couldn't think too hard about it, or I would start crying again, or screaming. Just me and Dad—well, I guess that's kind of the way it's been lately anyway.

"Cece, what do you think?" Dad asked.

I looked at my parents, sitting across the room from each other. My vision was blurred by the tears forming in my eyes. "Do you really want to know what I think?"

"Yes," they spoke at the same time.

"Okay," I said, as I stared at my father. "You're really selfish, Dad, and you don't *really* care what I think. You make your decisions based on what *you* think." I looked over at my mother, "and I guess this is perfect for you, Mom. Now you can spend all the time in the world at work and never have to see me and Dad." Those comments were the meanest things I had ever said. Speaking these hurtful words made me start crying. So I left the room, heading upstairs to grab Oscar for a walk.

When I came back down the stairs, my parents were still sitting in the living room. They were silent.

# CHAPTER FIVE

# THE REARVIEW MIRROR

The next two weeks flew by like a tornado—fast and completely out of control.

I'd never really had to pack before, so this was a very new experience. I barely knew what to do. To make it all a bit easier I made a list of everything I would need in Los Angeles. Then I organized everything with one giant cardboard box for each category of my stuff. I had a box that I labeled "tops," which included anything I wore on the top half of my body—hats too. Of course, I had a box labeled "bottoms" as well. This included everything I wore on the bottom half of my body—except for things I wore on my feet. I had a separate box labeled "feet." This was not because I am insane, it's just because I had too many shoes to fit in the "bottoms" box. I also had one entire box that was filled with snowboard stuff—I labeled that box "just in case."

Anyway, after about five hours, I filled the tenth and final box with my stuffed animals and my Three Special Things. For the record, I labeled that box "animals," which made me nervous because I was absolutely positive someone would think I had actually packed live animals in the box.

My entire life, twelve years, fit in those ten boxes. I guess that's because I don't keep very much stuff, throwing almost everything away to make my life neat and tidy. I've always kept my Three Special Things with me, though. It seems silly, but they are really important to me.

The first is a pair of Mom's glasses. Before Mom got laser eye surgery, she could barely see. Sometimes I put on her glasses and everything gets all fuzzy. I think of what it would be like to be a grown woman, like Mom, and see the world through her eyes.

The second special thing is an orange coated in plastic acrylic. I won it at the Wyoming State Fair when I was six years old. There was this booth at the fair that had a penny jar. Whoever guessed closest to how many pennies were in the jar won all the pennies *plus* a plastic-coated orange. There were 643 pennies in the jar. I guessed 637. The guy behind the booth told me that the orange inside the plastic coating really is an actual orange. It's a strange prize, I know, but it's the first thing I ever won.

The third special thing is a framed picture of my parents at their wedding. They're dancing. My dad is dipping my mom. Mom is wearing a big, beautiful, white wedding dress and Dad is wearing a horrible blue tuxedo that he swears was stylish at the time. They're both smiling and look so happy in the picture.

I'm not sure why I keep these things, I just do. I keep them in my nightstand drawer. No one but Oscar knows about my Three Special Things. It's just too embarrassing to tell anyone else how important they are to me.

When I finally finished boxing everything up, I walked around my empty room. There were grooves in the carpet from where my furniture had sat for the last twelve years. I sat on the carpet and ran my fingers along the lines. They were like sad and lonely snowboard tracks in the grey carpet. I sat there on the floor for about an hour, I guess. I wasn't thinking about anything in particular. I felt numb.

I probably would have been there forever if a nudge in my back hadn't snapped me out of it. I turned around and there was Oscar, standing there with one of my snowboarding gloves in his mouth. "Hey, boy," I said, scratching his ears. "Where'd you get that?" I took the glove from his mouth. "What a great idea."

Oscar barked once in response. I told you my dog is a genius, right?

The next thing I knew I was tearing apart the box labeled "just in case." I had to hit the slopes one last time before I left— *just in case* I never came back.

Fifteen minutes later, I was standing at the top of the Big Chill. I strapped on my binding like I'd done a million times before. This time it felt weird, though.

It was a perfect day to snowboard—the sun was shining and there was about a foot of new powder. Normally, I would be in heaven on a day like this. Not today, though. I couldn't shake this feeling I was having, as if I was losing something. I tried to ignore it as I stood up and began my run down the mountain.

The powder was up to my knees. The trees were covered in thick white blankets. Still, when the wind blew, I could catch a faint whiff of pine. I started to snap out of it as soon as I began to pick up speed. It was hard not to feel great when I was on the mountain. I was in total control up here. My board did exactly what I wanted it to do. I sliced through the snow like I was riding a giant razor. I was precise. I was even. I was a snowflake. I was totally alone. I was as light as the air. I floated down the mountain.

The tracks I left behind were in the shapes of perfect Cs, like my name. CC was here. CC was here. CC was here.

I took my time getting down the mountain. I was in the big bowl of the Big Chill, and I hung on to every turn as long as I could. I reached down and touched the snow with my glove. There was one thought running through my head like my favorite song on repeat—I love this mountain, I love this mountain, I love this mountain . . .

The next day was my last day of school in Rockville. It was actually pretty uneventful. I don't have any classes with Sally, so there weren't too many real friends to say goodbye to. Although she'd never admit it, I think Mrs. Cruickshank was actually glad to see me go. I was a big pain for her. I will miss Mr. Low, though. When science class ended he shook my hand and said, "Looks like Hollywood's getting a good doctor."

The weirdest thing about leaving school that day was that it didn't *feel* weird. It actually felt kind of good. I hadn't made very many close friends here. Besides Sally, most of the friends I had made were the ones I'd met on the mountain. I never quite felt like I fit in at school. In a way, I was glad to be leaving it behind. It was as if I'd gotten a free pass to start all over somewhere else. Not that I wanted to leave Wyoming, but maybe there was at least one good thing about moving. Maybe going to school in Los Angeles would be better for me.

That feeling lasted twenty-one hours. That's when my dad and I were leaving for good, and it was finally time to say goodbye to Sally for real. I was not looking forward to this. I got by most of the time by pretending it wasn't going to happen. I convinced myself that Sally was going to be moving with me. It was a good plan and it worked pretty well.

Mom, Dad, and I had loaded up the car. We rented one of those trailers that you put behind your car for our boxes and furniture. We didn't have too much stuff because the studio was helping furnish a house for us. Dad thought this was the greatest thing in the world.

We were all packed up when Sally walked up our driveway. "Cece," she said, "were you going to leave without saying good-bye?" She looked upset.

I guess I really had convinced myself that she was moving with me, because I actually *was* going to leave without saying good-bye. "No," I lied.

Sally looked at me blankly.

I smiled so I wouldn't cry. "So, where's *your* stuff?" I asked.

"Come on, Cece. That isn't funny. You know I'm not coming with you."

That's what did it. All the pretending and not thinking about it couldn't change what was going to happen. I was moving. Sally wasn't. The floodgates opened. All the sadness I was holding back and pretending wasn't there came out all at once. I started bawling right there in my driveway.

This set off Sally and she lost it too. We were falling apart in my front yard. I was doing those big heaving sobs and Sally was doing shorter ones that were not as drawn out as mine, but much louder.

"Sally . . . I'm . . . going . . . to . . . miss . . . you . . . so . . . much." I managed to get out between heaving and sobbing.

"It's not fair!" she sob-screamed back.

We hugged each other. My nose was running. Tears streamed down my face. We stayed that way for a while. Hugging and crying. Crying and hugging. Eventually, we calmed down and broke apart. I didn't know what to say. Sally reached into her pocket and pulled out a small round package. It was wrapped in shiny gold paper and tied with a red bow.

"What is it?" I asked, wiping the tears off my cheek with the palm of my hand.

Sally shrugged. "Open it later, okay?'

My dad opened the front door, holding a bag full of drinks and snacks. "Well, Cece, it's time to hit the road." He looked at Sally. "Do you want a ride home, Sally?"

"No thanks, Mr. Morgan. I'm going to head the park for a while."

A moment later, my mom came out the front door. She gave me a hug. "I'll see you soon. Things are going to be okay. You can do it." I was so upset that I couldn't say anything back to her.

Sally was still standing next to our car. I needed to leave right away or else I was going to lose it again, so I got in the car.

"Girls," my dad said, "I know it seems hard now, but Los Angeles isn't that far away. And, Sally, I spoke to your parents, and they've agreed to let you come and visit us there. We'll have a blast." I looked at Sally through the rolled down window and smiled. It was the best piece of news I'd heard since I found out we were moving. "You guys have too good a friendship to let a little distance

29

get in the way," my dad said. "It'll work out." When he wanted to, Dad could really make me feel better.

He opened the door and Oscar hopped into the backseat. Oscar flashed a little poodle smile to let me know that he was excited for the road trip. That makes one of us, I thought. We pulled out of the driveway and gave a final wave to Mom. Sally waved too. I couldn't turn back. Instead, I stared at the rearview mirror as we drove away. Dad honked a few times as my house, my mother, my town, and my best friend got smaller and smaller and smaller— until it all faded out of sight.

That's when I reached into my pocket and pulled out Sally's present. I unwrapped it carefully. At first, I didn't know what it was. It was a little round disc about the size of a coaster that you put drinks on, and it was wrapped in plastic. I flipped it over. The sticker on the back read: Mr. Fatty Waves Surf Wax. It was wax for a surfboard. There was a tiny card taped to the label. I opened it. "If you can't ride the mountains, you might as well ride the waves."

"What's that?" asked my Dad.

"Nothing," I said. I leaned back in the seat. As the road blurred by us and the car gently swayed back and forth from the strong Wyoming winds, I closed my eyes and

# CHAPTER SIX

# ENTERING LOS ANGELES

It took two days to get to California. Along the way we passed through the rest of Wyoming, most of Utah, and a little bit of Nevada. I slept through a lot of the ride, despite Dad blasting the radio and singing a few times. When I *was* up, Oscar and I usually just looked out the window. Everything around us was flat and that seemed to go on forever, especially on the second day of the trip in southern Utah and Nevada.

Everything changed when we got about an hour or so outside of Los Angeles. Things started to get more and more developed. We passed one suburban town after another. They all looked exactly alike. We passed the same stores with the same giant signs—probably selling the exact same stuff. The freeway kept getting wider, too. It seemed like every ten miles, another lane appeared. The wider the road got, the more cars there were on it. I had never seen so many cars. I felt trapped, sandwiched, between all the cars. I could tell my dad was getting nervous too. Years of driving in snow and ice hadn't prepared him for navigating through a ten-lane river of traffic.

The car climbed a pretty steep hill, and when we finally reached the top, we passed a sign that read: Entering Los Angeles, population three-million-six-hundred- ninety-four-thousand, eight hundred and twenty. Dad read it out loud, but when he read it, he added three more numbers to the total, three million, six-hundred-ninety-four thousand, eight hundred and twenty-three—now that he and Oscar and I had arrived. I laughed out loud. "That's almost six times the entire population of Wyoming." I said.

We drove about forty-five more minutes. Everywhere you looked, there were people and homes everywhere. There were houses and apartment buildings as far as I could see. They were next to stores, over freeways, on cliffs. They were everywhere. The roads were everywhere too. Back home, there were two main roads going through downtown. Here, there were too many stop-lights to count. The concrete went on forever.

We got off the freeway and stopped at an intersection that connected eight different roads. It was confusing. I was trying to help my dad with the map, but I couldn't read it. There were too many things to look at!

I stared out the window as we waited for the light to change. Next to a sports car stood a bearded homeless man with his hands on a shopping cart. He was begging for spare change. A flock of people on motor scooters passed us, as if a tiny motor scooter gang was the most normal thing in the world. Billboards in different languages were everywhere, advertising expensive cars, rap albums, and California cheese. Oscar was running around in circles in the back seat. His nose was going crazy with all the strange new smells.

I couldn't get over how fast the neighborhoods changed. We'd pass one block and all the apartments and houses would be run down with trash everywhere. Two blocks later, there'd be a bunch of fancy cars parked in front of nice buildings. How did everyone know where they were supposed to stay?

We eventually drove into a nice neighborhood that stayed nice. The further we went, the nicer the houses got. The street was lined with towering palm trees. This was what LA looked like in all the photographs I had seen, and in all the movies, too. I had to admit, it was beautiful.

My dad double-checked an address he had written down on a little piece of paper. He then made a left turn, and pulled up to a gate. He rolled down the window. "Here we are, Chili," he said, then punched some numbers into a little metal box in front of the gate. The gate swung open and we drove into a large round driveway. The only word I could use to describe what seemed to be our new house was "Whoa!"

I guess having a big time radio show pays off.

When we opened the front door, we were impressed right away. The house was beautiful. We took a look around before running back to the car to grab our overnight bags. Even though we were excited to finally be there, Dad and I both were just about ready to pass out. We decided to head to our bedrooms and get some sleep. We would explore the house more fully in the morning.

I had to admit it, my bedroom was awesome. It had high ceilings, and in the upper left corner, there was a skylight. Plus, it was huge! I measured it before I went to sleep. It was six paces wider on one side, and seven paces wider on the other side, than my old room. That might not sound like a very big deal, but go walk that many steps in your room, and you'll see how big it really is.

When I woke up that first morning, the sun was shining on the foot of my bed, a breeze was blowing and some birds were chirping. Even through the glass, I could feel the strength of the Los Angeles sun. Oscar loved it. He was lying at the foot of my bed, basking in the sunbeam from the skylight, panting softly and smiling. It was a great morning.

"You like the skylight?" I asked.

He thumped his tail, which means yes.

Besides the skylight, there are three windows in my room, two more than in my old room. One of the windows looks out into the backyard—which I quickly found out was absolutely beautiful. The first thing I noticed when I checked it out was the pool. I could not believe that we had our own pool! Light blue tiles lined the bottom, giving the water an almost fake, perfect, bright blue color. It was practically begging me to jump in. Normally, I prefer the frozen kind of water, but the pool looked so nice that I decided I might start to enjoy the liquid kind more.

While peering out the window, I noticed my Dad in the yard. He was in his bathing suit, staring at the water. He saw me watching him and waved. Then, he put down his coffee mug, and like a man possessed, ran into the pool and jumped in with a loud "whoo." He then splashed around like he was in heaven. I quickly threw on my suit and ran outside to join him. By the time I got out there, Oscar was swimming too. I had no idea he liked the water.

The temperature was perfect, just a little warmer than the outside air. I came up from under the water and Oscar swam towards me. It was a funny moment, being in a swimming pool with my dad and a big silver poodle.

I glanced around the yard as I floated toward Dad. We had a lot of lemon trees, which not only looked cool, but smelled fantastic. Plus, there were all kinds of tropical looking flowers in front of the lemon tress. Hanging from one of the lemon trees was a hummingbird feeder. So far, I had seen four hummingbirds. They are amazing. They look like they are standing still in midair because their wings flap so fast that you can't even see them flapping. When I spoke to Sally later that day, the first thing I told her about was the hummingbirds.

That weekend in our new house was great. Dad, Oscar, and I had a really good time. I even forgot for a little while that I was mad. Oscar loved the whole backyard, but the pool was his favorite. I also really loved being in the water. Although I swam a lot in Rockville, it was always in a big, crowded indoor pool.

I put off thinking about attending a new school on Monday. I used my old trick, convincing myself that I wouldn't have to go for a while. Deep down, I knew I was going to have to face the music eventually. I knew it wasn't going to be easy. Being the new kid isn't easy for anyone, but I knew it would be extra hard for me. I'd barely made any friends at my old school, and I'd lived in Rockville my whole life.

Before I knew it, Sunday night arrived. School was less than twelve hours away. I stood in my room, looking into the empty backyard. In the dark, the trees looked like one big shadow. The lights in the pool made a wavy kind of light that crept across the entire yard. It was warm, but a cool breeze flowed through my hair from my open window. It felt good. I was doing my best to try and be calm about tomorrow. Maybe Los Angeles wasn't going to be that bad.

# CHAPTER SEVEN

## NEW SCHOOL DISASTER

My hopes of things being better than I thought were flushed down the toilet like the goldfish I won at the winter carnival last year. I have to say, some people in LA are not like my backyard. They are not calm and peaceful. They are not nice and pretty. They are mean and ugly.

Anyway, here's what happened. I tried to be excited about the first day of school like my dad kept begging me to be. But it was really hard. Even getting dressed was stressful. First, I un- packed all my clothes and spread them all over my room. I laid out as many different possible outfits with the clothes I had as I could. Then I looked at these combinations—on the bed, on the chairs, on the floor—and realized that my Wyoming clothes might not be right for Los Angeles. There was nothing wrong with them—they just weren't LA. All I mean is, there wasn't anything special, re- vealing, or outrageous about them. Oscar watched as I walked back and forth between outfits, staring at one, staring at another.

"What do you think boy?" I asked holding up a pair of khaki pants and a striped pink and yellow shirt. This was one of my coolest shirts back home. He shook his head in disapproval. In matters of fashion, always listen to a standard poodle.

"Yeah, I know. I don't know what to do, though."

I obsessed about it until the very last minute. In the end, I decided my simplest outfit would probably be best. I would go with a white v-neck t-shirt and my best jeans. I figured maybe if I couldn't fit in, I should be as invisible as possible.

My first day started off well enough. All the kids seemed to be in their own worlds. No one paid much attention to me. But it was hard for me not to pay attention to them. Students at David Hasselhoff Middle School looked so different from the kids from Wyoming, I couldn't believe I was the same age as they were. Most girls wore tight shirts that showed their stomachs and lots of makeup too. They looked like they could have been in college. Most of the boys wore big baggy pants and had hair so spiky it looked like weapons.

My first class of the day was English, my least favorite subject. Despite what I thought going into class, my teacher, Mrs. Blossom, was really cool. She was younger than any teacher I've ever had. Her hair was dark brown with cool blonde streaks running though it. She smiled at me when I walked in. "You must be Cecelia. Welcome to David Hasselhoff and welcome to English."

"Thank you," I said. "You can call me Cece."

"I'm glad you're here a little early, Cece. I'd like to introduce you to the class, but I wanted to make sure you were cool with the introduction. No sense embarrassing you on the first day, right?" She smiled at me again. I never had a teacher who talked like Mrs. Blossom. She talked liked a kid. I felt comfortable with her right away. "So, you just moved here from Wisconsin, right?"

"Wyoming," I corrected her.

"Great. What do you think of LA so far?"

"It's a lot different from home," I said. "It seems like it never ends."

"It took me a few years to get used to it here. But if you give it a chance, it'll grow on you."

"I hope so."

The bell rang. I was so focused on talking to Mrs. Blossom that I didn't realize the class had filled up with kids. "I guess we should get started," said Mrs. Blossom, giving me a little wink. She showed me my seat. To my right was a skinny African American guy named Hershel who couldn't stop smiling. I knew his name was Hershel because it was stitched into the collared shirt he was wearing. He made eye contact with me the moment he walked in. I could tell right away that he had the most friend potential of anyone I had seen—though I had only been in homeroom so far.

Mrs. Blossom's class began. "All right people, we've got lots to do today. Before we start, I'd like to introduce you to a new student—Cece Morgan. How about giving Cece a nice welcome?"

The whole class shouted, "Welcome, Cece!"

I turned a little red, but for a good type of embarrassment.

"Cece just moved here from Wyoming," said Mrs. Blossom. "So you can imagine how big of a change Los Angeles is for her. I know that we'll all give an extra-special effort to make her feel welcome."

Hershel turned to me with another huge smile, "I think I speak for the entire class when I bid you farewell to Wyoming, the

38

Cowboy State, and bring you the sunniest of welcomes to California, the Golden State." I smiled from ear to ear. Hershel was definitely strange, but he was super nice.

For the rest of the class, Mrs. Blossom talked about adverbs. Now, normally, I would be in agony, but Mrs. Blossom was a great teacher. Even though she was talking about really boring stuff, the class paid attention as if she were giving a lesson on video games.

A single girl sitting in the back corner of the room, though, seemed completely bored. She was picking at her fingernails. I noticed that each nail was painted a different shade of pink. I didn't even know that there were ten shades of pink. She was dressed in the same tiny-shirt outfit that seemed to be the uniform here.

She must have noticed me looking at her, because she looked up from her nails and made eye contact with me. She narrowed her eyes and glared. Her icy stare made me want to crawl deep inside my backpack and never come out. I quickly turned away from her. I could tell this was the kind of person you didn't want to mess with, and, without meaning to, I had just gotten on her bad side.

The class ended and I stood in the hall trying to find room 204. Just then, I felt a hard tap on my shoulder. When I turned around Ms. Perfect Pretty Pink Nails was standing a few feet away from me. "Why were you staring at me in class?" she asked rudely.

"Excuse me?"

"I asked you why you were staring at me. Are you hard of hearing or just stupid?"

"No, um, I'm not," I said, totally shocked by this comment.

"Not what? Hard of hearing, or stupid?"

By this time, a small crowd had gathered around Ms. Perfect Pretty Pink Nails and me. This was not what I needed on my first day. I started to get really nervous. Why was this girl picking on me? I didn't do anything to her. "Neither," I managed to get out.

"So then, why were you staring at me?"

I didn't know what she wanted from me. "I'm not sure what you want from me." I confessed.

"I want you to tell me what makes you think you have the right to come here from the middle of nowhere and act like you can do whatever you want. Things are different here, Ms. Wyoming."

"Oh, okay," I said. I stood there helplessly. I didn't know what to do or where to go. "I'll keep that in mind." I said, as I tried to walk away.

She stood in front of me. There was no escaping her. "So," she continued, "what are we going to do about our little problem here?"

"I don't really think we have a problem," I said, trying to diffuse the situation. "What we have is a misunderstanding."

She got right up in my face. "No, we definitely have a problem, Wyoming freak! You show up here in your horrible clothes, and your stupid bag, and your stupid hair, and act like you can do whatever you want. You really are stupid!"

It was then that I did the worst possible thing I could have done. I started crying—right in front of everyone on my first day of school. And, of course, she did what all mean people do when someone starts crying—she laughed. A small crowd of girls who looked, and dressed exactly like Ms. Perfect Pretty Pink Nails joined her. I didn't know what to do. I felt trapped. I was certain that I was going to be standing here forever, crying in front of these horrible girls.

"Portia, what's going on here?" I heard an adult voice through the crowd.

Ms. Perfect Pretty Pink Nails' smile turned to a look of panic. Mrs. Blossom made her way through all of the kids who'd gathered around me.

"Nothing, Mrs. Blossom," said Ms. Perfect Pretty Pink Nails, or I guess Portia, which seemed like the perfect name for her.

"This looks like a little more than nothing," said Mrs. Blossom. She watched me wipe the tears on my check away with my palm. Her face became angry.

"It's okay, Mrs. Blossom." I spoke up. "I'm just homesick. It's a lot different here in Los Angeles. Portia didn't do anything."

Portia looked at me like I was crazy. I could tell Mrs. Blossom didn't believe my words, but I think she knew what I was trying to do. If I got Portia into trouble right then, she would make the rest of my life in Los Angeles miserable. I was just trying to get her off my back.

"Well," said Mrs. Blossom doubtfully, "if there are any problems, you can talk to me anytime, Cece. I don't like to see people having trouble at school."

"Thank you," I said forcing a smile.

By this time, most people had cleared away and I was able to walk to my next class. But I didn't. Instead, I marched straight into the girls' bathroom and opened up the first stall, locking it behind me. To my relief, the bathroom was empty. Sitting there alone, I got the rest of my crying out.

# CHAPTER EIGHT

# THE MAGICIAN

My crying was interrupted when I heard someone enter the bathroom. Footsteps echoed on the tiled floor, getting closer to my stall. I heard someone call my name, "Cece?" How did anyone here know my name? And how did anyone know I was in the bathroom? And why did it sound like a boy's voice?

"Cece?" I heard the voice again.

The voice definitely didn't belong to Portia, so I answered. "Yeah."

"It's me, Hershel, from English class. Are you okay?"

"What are you doing in here?" I asked, as I opened the door. "This is the girl's room."

"You're upset. I thought I'd try to make you feel better." Hershel answered me as if standing in the girls' bathroom was the most normal thing in the world. I figured I didn't have much to lose. At least he wasn't Portia.

"Why do you care so much?" I asked, defensively.

"Because," he whispered, "you probably won't believe this, but a year ago, when I first moved here, I used to get picked on." He paused, then raised his voice a bit, "They were picking on Hershel, last year. And it really sucked. So, I know how you're feeling—not excellent." Then, without saying another word, he reached into his pocket and pulled out a deck of cards. He fanned them out in front of me. "Pick a card," he said.

"Excuse me?" I asked.

"Pick a card," he said again, holding his hand over his eyes. "But don't show me."

I did as Hershel said. He grinned at me as I pulled an eight of diamonds from the deck.

"Got your card?"

I nodded.

"Excellent, now put it back in the deck, anywhere in the deck. Careful, don't show me what it is. The magic doesn't work if I see where you put it."

I put the card back in the deck.

Hershel shuffled the cards. "I'm shuffling the cards here. Now if I could pick your card from this single shuffle, it would be impressive. But for you, I'm going for mind-bending amazing." Hershel handed me the deck of cards. "Now I'm going to turn around and I'd like you to shuffle the cards without me looking."

He turned around and I shuffled the deck a few times.

"Are you finished?" Hershel asked.

"All done," I said.

Hershel turned around and I handed him the shuffled cards.

"If I could pick out your card now, you'd have to agree that it would be mind-bending, right?"

"Right," I smiled.

"But if I was able to pick your card after doing *this*. . . " Hershel dropped the cards onto the bathroom floor. He spread the cards around with his hands. "It would arguably be the most excellent trick in the galaxy, right?"

It would certainly be the most disgusting trick in the galaxy, I thought. "Right."

Hershel gathered up the cards from the bathroom floor. I really hoped he wasn't going to make me touch the cards again. He shuffled through the deck for what seemed like five minutes. He finally stopped. "Prepare to be dazzled," he said as he flashed a three of clubs in my face.

"That's not my card," I said.

"That's impossible," replied Hershel.

"I'm sorry, but that's not my card." I was laughing now.

"Of course that's not your card." He smiled mischievously. "What you just witnessed was the showmanship known only to a true magician."

Once again, Hershel fumbled through the cards. He pulled another card from the deck—a ten of hearts. "Stupendous, right?"

"That's not my card either," I said again.

"Hmmm," said Hershel. "This must be a rare case where I can't read my participant's mind. Being in the girls' bathroom must be interfering somehow."

"Must be," I said.

"Anyway," said Hershel, putting the deck of cards back in his pocket. "Don't let Portia get to you. There are plenty of nice people here."

"Thanks, Hershel," I said. I smiled at him again. I wanted

to give him a hug, because he had been so nice, but I decided not to. Hershel looked like the kind of guy, that if you hugged him in the girls' bathroom, he would kind of freak out.

"It's my pleasure." He bowed. "Hershel the famous magician is late for class." And with that, he left the bathroom.

A few minutes later, I left the bathroom too. Thanks to Hershel, I was feeling much better now. But it lasted only about three seconds. That's how long it was before Portia stood in front of me again in the hallway. "Hey, freak, where do you think you're going?"

"Art," I said.

"Well, before you go, I don't want you getting the wrong idea."

"What do you mean?"

"Just because you got Blossom off my back doesn't mean that I like you any more."

Again, I found myself not knowing what to say.

"We had enough freaks here before you showed up." Portia leaned in so close to my face that I could smell her. She pushed her finger into my chest, "I'm going to make sure that you never get comfortable, freak." Then she started to walk away. As she made her way down the hallway, she turned back toward me and yelled, "I can't wait to see what you wear tomorrow."

She walked away, laughing with her friends. It was amazing how a complete stranger could make me feel so bad about myself. The next thing I knew I was back in the bathroom crying. I wished that Hershel knew a magic trick that would make Portia disappear.

# CHAPTER NINE

# THE BIG BLUE OCEAN

My dad was waiting for me when school finally got out. The bell rang at three thirty. I felt like I was being released from prison. He sat in the driver's seat with a giant grin on his face. After we left the parking lot and began the drive home, Dad turned to me and asked, "How was it?"

Seeing him sitting there with that big, stupid grin made me lose it. "It was the worst day of my entire life!" I screamed at him.

"What happened?" he asked, slowing the car to a stop on the side of the road.

"Why would you care?" I snapped at him.

"Come on, Chili, I want to know what happened."

"No you don't. You just want me to be quiet so that you don't have to feel guilty about making me move here. I told you I was going to hate it here, and you know something, I was wrong. They hate me here. We're not supposed to be here, Dad." I was yelling and crying at the same time. I couldn't hold back. "I want to go back home!"

"I'm sorry you had such a terrible day. Will you please tell me about it?"

"You're not sorry enough to move back, are you?"

"Honey, you have to give it more than one day."

"Why? I know it's not going to get better. I'm never going to fit in here. I don't want to fit in here!"

We drove in silence for a few minutes. I could tell Dad wanted to talk, but he didn't know what to say. I closed my eyes, wishing that things were different. Dad broke the silence. "I have an idea—let's go see the ocean." There was desperation in his voice as he spoke. "Maybe that will make you feel a little better."

We drove in silence for a while, immersed in an endless sea of cars, concrete, and palm trees. Outside of the car, the air was filled with the whooshing sound of cars passing us and the occasional honk. Twenty minutes later, we ended up at a parking lot with a big sign that read: Dolly Parton State Park. Everything in Los Angeles seemed to be named after a celebrity, and to be honest, it was starting to bother me. Everything was starting to bother me.

When we got out of the car I noticed right away that the air was different. It smelled cleaner than the air outside of David Hasselhoff Middle School—and it had a taste. It was salty. Right away, I could feel something inside of me change. It was weird. The frustration, sadness, and anger that had overwhelmed me a moment earlier took a back seat to my curiosity about the ocean. I tried to hide it from my father, but I was genuinely excited to be there at Dolly Parton State Park.

I took another deep breath and stood on my tip-toes to catch a glimpse of the ocean. I couldn't see it yet because of a big pile of sand in front of the parking lot. Just smelling the air, and hearing the waves crashing again and again in the distance made my heart beat quickly. Then, out of nowhere, I kicked off my shoes and started running toward the giant sand dune that stood between me and the giant ocean. I surprised even myself with this sudden burst of energy. Dad was wearing his nice clothes from his big day at the studio, but quickly flipped off his shoes and socks and darted up the hill behind me.

The sand made me run slowly. My feet sunk a few inches with every step I took. I felt a little like I was walking in deep snow. I liked the familiar—yet different—feeling. As I reached the top of the sand pile a step before my dad, I caught a glimpse of a big blue something that wasn't sky. It was the ocean. Now, I had seen the ocean on television before, and once on an airplane I flew over the ocean, but I had never actually seen it up close. It was amazing!

"Well Chili, there it is." Dad said, making a visor with his right hand as he reached the top.

"Wow!" I stared at the surf. "Those waves are awesome." We walked a little farther down the sand mound toward the water. I was mesmerized. The blue went on forever. There was no other side. It was one big, beautiful thing, and it was alive. I felt alive just watching it. A wave would crash against the shore then return to the sea. Then another would come in. And another. And another. It never ended.

Even though the ocean looked nothing like a mountain, I felt much the same way as when I stood above an untracked run of fresh powder. I didn't feel sad. I wasn't even mad at my dad. I felt calm. I was just watching the ocean. I was totally happy.

"Think about it, Chili," said my dad, "somewhere in Japan,

a dad and his daughter could be standing on the shores looking out at the same ocean."

I looked out at the endless blue. I thought about Japan. I wondered if that girl was mad at her father too. I wondered if he might be some famous Japanese radio personality, and maybe she was a killer snowboarder from the mountains of Japan. Maybe they just moved to some beach town in Japan and she was checking out the ocean for the first time. Maybe earlier in the day, she had been crying in a bathroom stall. Maybe there was a girl at her school named Portia—or the Japanese equivalent to Portia. And maybe today was the worst day of her life too. I thought about her for a few minutes and felt a little better.

Staring out at the ocean made my mind wander. I started to think about Oscar and how I was sure that he would like the ocean. I bet he'd like Japan, for that matter. I pictured him in the ocean and smiled. In the middle of these random thoughts, something in the water caught my attention. I squinted at a group of people about a hundred yards out. I walked closer to the water. Dad followed right behind me.

When I figured out that they were surfing, my heart started to really race. "Wow," I said again, loudly, into the air. Then I watched powerful waves coming in and the skilled surfers coming in with them. It was so cool—they were riding the waves. They were riding the ocean. It reminded me of snowboarding, and I felt another jolt of excitement. This was the best I had felt since we got here.

"I've got to try that," I whispered, quiet enough so Dad wouldn't hear.

One surfer in particular caught my attention—a woman in a black and orange wetsuit. She was so graceful, catching one wave

49

after another. She stayed on the waves much longer than everyone else, turning and finding ways to make her rides go one seemingly forever. She carved big Cs with her board—CC, CC, CC—spelling out my name like I did when I was snowboarding. I wanted to be like her. I wanted to be like this woman who was waving at me. This woman was waving at me? Why was this woman waving at me?

"Do you know that lady?" asked my dad.

"I don't think so."

She paddled on her board to shore and walked up to us. As she got closer, I recognized her. It was Mrs. Blossom. Oh my gosh! She looked much different in a wetsuit than she did wearing a dress in class. "Hey, Cece," she said, wringing water out of her hair.

"Hi, Mrs. Blossom," I said. "Dad, this is my English teacher, Mrs. Blossom."

My dad looked a little surprised. In Wyoming, I don't think he'd ever seen any of my teachers in wetsuits. "Hello. I'm Marty Morgan," he held out his hand. They shook. "It's a pleasure to meet you."

"You look really great out there, Mrs. Blossom," I said.

"Thanks," she said. "The waves are pretty choice today."

"Do you surf a lot?" I asked.

"As often as I can." She cleared her throat, "You know, Cece, we have a surf club at school. I encourage all my students to surf. There's nothing else like it on the planet."

"It looks like a lot of fun. The surf club sounds cool, too." I said.

Mrs. Blossom smiled and brushed back her wet hair from

her forehead. "We meet every Wednesday and Thursday afternoon, and Saturday morning. Beginners are welcome."

"That sounds great," Dad said.

I was actually getting excited about this surfing idea. "Yeah," I said.

"We've got extra wetsuits and a board you can borrow while you're learning. Just bring a bathing suit with you to school. It will be great." Mrs. Blossom looked back out at the ocean. "Well, I'm heading back in before the waves get too blown out. See you tomorrow, Cece. Nice meeting you," she said to my dad.

"Nice meeting you." Dad waved.

We watched her run back out into the ocean and paddle through the waves. Before we knew it, she was surfing again. Seeing Mrs. Blossom surf, and thinking about learning to surf myself, made me completely forget about how mad I was at my dad. I even forget about Portia, at least for a few minutes, anyway.

# CHAPTER TEN

## SURF'S UP

The next Wednesday finally arrived, my first day participating in Surf Club. I was really eager to get on a surf board. When I had closed my eyes the night before, I imagined myself surfing. I was carving big, beautiful turns, like I did when I was on the mountain. I just knew I was going to be a natural surfer.

Before school, I crammed my green bathing suit, a towel, a pair of shorts, and a t-shirt, along with Sally's Mr. Fatty Wave's Surf Wax, into my book bag. I was actually excited about going to school.

Despite my enthusiasm, school was as horrible as usual. Portia and her crew were determined to make me miserable. Today, Mrs. Blossom handed back our English papers, and Portia noticed the A I got on my homework. As I walked out of class, she remarked, "Maybe you should spend a little less time thinking about getting A's and a little more time thinking about how you look."

"Yeah," one of her wannabes chimed in.

"I mean, your shirt is disgusting!" The girl who said that was wearing the *exact* same shirt as Portia.

I don't know if I had reached my limit, or built up a tolerance to Portia—maybe I was just too excited about surfing—but whatever the reason, Portia couldn't get to me. "Excuse me," I said as I walked though Portia and her idiot friends. I had more important things to do than be upset about what they thought of me. For the first time since I arrived in Los Angeles two weeks ago, I had gone through an entire day without crying in the bathroom. I know that sounds awful, but at least I was making progress.

When the bell rang, I hurried to the parking lot. A bunch of kids were standing around in shorts and t-shirts. I didn't recognize most of them but I immediately spotted Hershel.

"Hi, Hershel," I said.

Hershel stuck out his hand and I shook it. "Cece, so glad you could make it this beautiful Wednesday afternoon," he smiled.

"I didn't know you surfed," I said.

"Oh yes," said Hershel. "I fence as well, head up the math team, and am starting a Moon Appreciation Club next semester. You just have to love the moon. It's big, round, and it lights up the night sky. It's excellent. I'll send you an e-mail about it."

"Cool," was the only reply I could come up with.

I stood with Hershel as all the other surfers talked in their own little groups. A few minutes passed and then Mrs. Blossom pulled up in a big white van. She stopped, jumped out, and opened the passenger door for us. "Next stop, tasty waves!" she said with a gigantic smile.

We all piled in the van. I was excited. It was the same kind of excitement I used to feel on rides up to the mountain before snowboarding—the anticipation of good times ahead. The van moved a few feet and then stopped suddenly. The side door opened again. My heart sank as Portia and two of her clones climbed in. They made a boy get out of a seat so that they could all sit together. At least they aren't sitting near me, I thought.

As soon as the wheels on the van starting rolling for real, Hershel started talking. Wow, could he talk. At first, I did my best to listen. "Cece, the future in the pet industry lies not in dogs or cats, but in robotic monkeys. Think about it. It's a robot. It's a monkey. It's excellent. I've written a number of letters to both pet companies and robotic companies. I'm confident this idea will break soon. I mean, can you imagine an animal with the smarts of a monkey that never has to use the bathroom?" He paused, but I didn't know what to say. "I call them chimpanpleases."

After getting through his chimpanplease idea, I started to pay only half-attention to what Hershel was saying. It wasn't that he was bothering me—I just couldn't keep up with his mouth. Luckily, he didn't seem to notice that I had faded out. He kept right on talking. The other half of my attention wandered around the van. I recognized some faces from the halls, two girls from my art class, and a guy I had gym with. Some people, though, I had never seen before.

I noticed two boys sitting near Portia who were talking. I knew I shouldn't be looking in her direction, but something made me keep looking—particularly at the boy on the left. As he spoke, he moved his hands up and down like he was imitating waves. Even from halfway across the van, I caught glimpses of his eyes. They were deep blue, like the waves I imagined he was talking about. His eyes stood out against his dark brown hair and tanned skin.

He must have noticed me looking at him, because he turned around and his eyes met mine. I instantly felt two things: embarrassment and a jolt of excitement. He looked at me! He noticed me. This was good. But, he noticed me because I was staring at him like a weirdo. This was bad. Our eyes met for a second time. He smiled. That little jolt of excitement turned into a lightening bolt. I could feel my face turning a shade of a tomato red. I quickly looked away and rejoined Hershel's talking marathon. "Just imagine the possibilities of a popsicle that stays cold but won't melt. It will change that way we think about frozen items on sticks."

"That sounds like a good idea, Hershel," I said, pretending like nothing had happened.

"Thanks. Yeah, I think so too."

Hershel stopped talking. "Are you okay, Cece? Your face is all red."

"Oh yeah, I'm fine. I just get a little flushed sometimes." I lied.

Hershel went right back to talking after that.

We eventually arrived at Dolly Parton State Park, the same beach where I'd seen Mrs. Blossom surfing. I did my best to keep my distance from the boy with the blue eyes. And of course, I stayed away from Portia. It wasn't that difficult with Hershel by my side. His mouth never seemed to get tired. He was the perfect barrier. "We surf here because there's an offshore sandbar about two miles out that produces consistently excellent waves. Plus, there's a sandy bottom here, which believe me, is what you want when you wipe out." We followed Mrs. Blossom from the parking lot onto the sand. Even as it became harder to walk, Hershel's mouth didn't slow down. "Some beaches along the coast have rocky shores, which produce some great waves. But if you fall off your board when the water's too shallow you're hamburger meat. Not excellent."

From snowboarding, I knew what it was like having to stay on a board at the right time. I was going to be fine. Hershel kept on talking as we walked. We climbed the little sand hill, and the big beautiful ocean came into view. I felt the same excitement that I did the other day when I looked at the waves crashing into the shore, one after the other.

We approached a little pink hut in the middle of the beach. Mrs. Blossom looked up at the hut and shielded the sun with her hands. "Hi, Pam," she said.

A tanned face with sunglasses leaned down. "Hey, Sonya." I guess Mrs. Blossom's first name was Sonya.

I had never seen a real-life lifeguard before. I mean, there were lifeguards at the pools I used to swim in back home, but they were always nerdy high school kids who were monitoring a four-foot deep pool with no waves. This was completely different.

Pam walked down the ramp to meet Mrs. Blossom. I stared at her as she approached us. Her chiseled arms and legs looked like they'd been carved from stone. She reminded me of a Doberman Pinscher—all muscle and no fat. She definitely wasn't a poodle. Her hair was short and slicked back. If she'd worn a cape, I would have believed she could fly. Yes, I was impressed.

Pam opened a padlocked door under the lifeguard shack. Inside was a bunch of surfboards and wetsuits. "Suit up!" she said, and everyone made a mad rush grabbing boards and wetsuits. I didn't know what to do, so I just stood there.

"Cece," said Mrs. Blossom, "we have a beginner's board

I start all my new surfers on." She disappeared and came out with a gigantic board and a wetsuit. "I know this looks pretty clunky, but it's really the best way to learn."

I studied the board for a second. It was this monstrous faded green foam board. I looked over at the other kids suiting up. My board was at least twice as big as theirs. I thought about telling Mrs. Blossom about how good of a snowboarder I was. I wanted to let her know that even though I'd never surfed before, I was definitely going to be good enough to start on a better board. Then I thought twice about it, deciding to *wow* everyone on this easy board instead.

Soon, each of my classmates was suited up and had a surf-board. Hershel was wearing this neon blue wetsuit that was probably two sizes too big for him and made him look like he had gigantic muscles—a bright blue bodybuilding surfer. It was so funny, but Hershel knew it too and was doing all these fake weightlifting poses. Everyone was laughing. You just had to love Hershel.

"Surf's up!" said Mrs. Blossom. "Everyone make sure that you can see Pam at all times. If you can't see her, she can't see you. Now, what do you say we go ride the ocean?"

Everyone ran excitedly to the shore. I felt a jab on my shoulder. I turned around and there was Portia. "Stay out of my way, loser," she hissed.

I didn't say anything back to her. I just waited for her to leave. Once she was a safe distance away I started lugging the giant green board towards the water.

Mrs. Blossom called after me, "Cece, before you go out, let's have a quick lesson."

I stopped. The rest of the class was already in the ocean.

They started paddling on their surfboards. I really wanted to be out there. "Do you really think I need a lesson? I mean, I've done a ton of snowboarding in my life. And I watched you surf before. So I think I'll get the hang of it."

Mrs. Blossom laughed. "Trust me, Cece, we should have a quick lesson. Surfing is different from anything you've ever done. I'm sure you'll be great out there, we just need to go over a few things."

"Okay," I sighed.

"Put your board on the sand," said Mrs. Blossom.

I put the huge green board on the sand.

"Do you have any questions before we begin?"

"No," I said. I didn't think that it was necessary to tell Mrs. Blossom this was my first time in the ocean. I had always been a great swimmer. I even swam across Trout Lake with my dad and Sally last summer.

"All right, I'll start by telling you that catching a wave is one of the hardest things for a beginner to learn. Once you get the wave, I'm sure you'll be able to ride it great, but getting on for the first time is tricky. It takes a lot of practice, and it takes learning the ocean. You see, waves come in sets. Some waves in the set are better than others. Some sets are better than others. Learning which wave to try to catch and where to go to get the best ones takes time to learn. It takes a lot of practice and patience. So don't be discouraged if you don't get it right away."

I felt like this was the same speech Mrs. Blossom gave every time she taught someone how to surf. I mean, I understood what she was saying, I just didn't think it applied to me. *I* was an athlete.

Mrs. Blossom had me lie down on the board and then push my arms down and jump up to my feet. She had me do this over and over again. Once I was standing on the board, I was amazed at how wide it was. It was at least three times wider than my snowboard. "You don't have much time to get up on your board once you get in a wave. You always have to be ready. Standing up has to become second nature to you," she said. She had me jump up a few more times. Finally she gave me the green light I was waiting for. "So, you ready to go and get some waves?"

I nodded.

"Hey, Pam," she shouted. "Will you keep one of your eyes on Cece in the shallows?"

"No problem." Pam's voice was firm and strong.

Mrs. Blossom turned back to me. "I need you to stay right there in front of Pam." Mrs. Blossom pointed to the area of water in front of the lifeguard shack.

"Okay," I said. I was glad that Mrs. Blossom was going to leave me alone, but I wished Pam the Lifeguard wouldn't be watching me. She made me nervous.

"Well, surf's up!" said Mrs. Blossom. She grabbed her board and ran for the water.

I grabbed the big green monster and followed her into the ocean.

# CHAPTER ELEVEN

## COLLISION COURSE

I walked up to the shoreline. It was hard to move, lugging that board. It felt like I was carrying twenty snowboards. A wave came in and got me wet up to my shins. I shuddered and took a deep breath. The water was freezing and I wasn't prepared for it. I looked up and saw the rest of the class further out, having fun. I watched Hershel gracefully ride a small wave. I was surprised how good he was.

Once I was up to my knees, I got on top of the board and paddled my arms like Mrs. Blossom taught me on the beach. Okay, so this is the ocean, I thought to myself. It's no big deal. It's just a big salty lake. I paddled a few strokes and then a bunch of white foamy water came rushing towards me. I tried as hard as I could to paddle through it, but the white water crashed into my face and knocked me backward and off the board. I was shocked by how powerful the water was. And these were only three-foot waves! I couldn't imagine the force behind a ten-footer.

A bunch of salty water went up my nose. It tasted disgusting. I love the taste of fresh snow, but fresh ocean is just plain gross—ugh! Now I was cold too, really cold. Maybe the ocean isn't as much like a lake as I thought. I stood up and got back on the green giant. Then I started paddling again. Getting knocked off the board had scared me a little bit. Still, I knew I could handle this. I mean, I've won forty-six races!

More white foam came barreling down at me. I fell off the board again and even more water went up my nose. Before I had the chance to be upset about falling off again, I felt a distracting tug at my leg. Was something attacking me? I whipped around as fast as I could and braced myself for a face-to-face encounter with an angry great white shark. All I saw, though, was the great green board trying to float back to shore. The leash around my ankle held it back. That was the tug.

I stood in the water for a moment and collected myself. At least I was warmer now. Mrs. Blossom had said that my wetsuit would be cold for a minute or two before the layer of water next to my skin warmed up. She was right. "Come on Cece, this is easy," I said to myself. Sure, I was off to a rocky start, but I was going to get the hang of this. Once again, I climbed on top of the green giant and started paddling. Once again, more whitewater came rushing toward me. This time, though, I put my arms down at the end of the board. I put my head down too, closing my eyes as water crashed over me. When I opened my eyes I was still on my board. Ha! I knew I was going to be good at this!

I paddled out a few more strokes to where some small waves were forming. I knew I wasn't supposed to get in front of anyone's wave, which wasn't going to be a problem because they were all so far away from me. It was the same etiquette as in snowboarding. You don't want to hang out at the bottom of a jump unless you want someone landing on you. In surfing, you don't want to cut in front of someone's ride unless you want to get plowed over.

I was surprised how much lighter the green giant was in the water than on the ground. It was pretty easy to move around, too. I finally paddled past the break, arriving at the spot where the waves were forming. Right when I got there, I spotted a nice one in the distance. I paddled to try and catch it. By the time I made it, though, it was gone and another was forming back where I'd just been a few seconds ago. I felt like the ocean was playing keep-away from me. I got back to my first spot, and missed another wave.

"Don't go out too far!" a booming voice cried, nearly scaring me to death.

I looked to the shore and saw Pam. She had a megaphone. The tone of her voice told me that she meant business. Pam was not someone to be ignored. So, instead of swimming out again, I stayed put and hoped that some waves would come my way. I didn't have to wait very long. A small wave came towards me. Quickly, I turned the board around and started paddling like crazy. I paddled and paddled but felt the wave go right under me and head to the shore without the green giant or me on it. "Well, I'll catch the next one," I said out loud, trying to hide the frustration in my voice, even though I was talking to myself.

I turned away from the shore to watch for another wave. A few seconds later, I was paddling like crazy again. And again I felt the wave pass under me without taking me with it. I didn't know what I was doing wrong. I was paddling as hard and as fast as I could. I tried to catch three more waves with the same result. I simply couldn't figure it out.

The rest of the class was bobbing up and down like a bunch of buoys—catching wave after wave and riding them into shore. I watched the boy with the blue eyes. He effortlessly paddled when a wave came, got caught in the wave, then stood up and carved beautiful turns in the ocean. He made it look so easy.

I hated to admit it, but even Portia was pretty good. How could she do this and I couldn't? It didn't make any sense. Didn't the ocean know how good at snowboarding I was?

I decided that there had to be something wrong with my board. Maybe the fin on the bottom needed to be replaced. That thought led me to smile. Yup, that's all this is— my board is defective. The board had been sitting so long, that no one had noticed that it was broken. I was getting all worked up over nothing.

I looked over to find Mrs. Blossom and let her know about my board. She was on a wave, making these long arching turns. I didn't want to interrupt her surfing just to fix my board, so I decided that I'd keep trying on the green giant. If I could learn to surf on a defective board, I bet I could surf anything after that.

"Aloha from the ocean," said a voice from out of nowhere. I turned around. "Hershel, you scared me."

"My apologies," said Hershel. He looked like a superhero in his bright blue wetsuit. It helped that he was wearing a neon purple swim-cap. "I just wanted to see how things were going with my aquatic friend and her first time on a surfboard."

"It's going okay, I guess. I'm having a little trouble with the board, though. I think it might be defective or something."

Hershel started laughing pretty hard. "A defective foam

board? That is excellent, Cece. Very funny."

"What do you mean?" I asked.

Hershel stopped laughing. His eyebrows and swim cap wrinkled. "You mean you're not kidding?"

"Why would I be kidding?"

"Well, that tremendous piece of foam is indestructible." Hershel started talking in that long way I've come to expect from him, "the durable nature of the board is what makes it such a breeze to ride. I can tell you for absolute certain that your board is not defective. Anyway, you think you're ready to come and try some bigger waves?" he asked.

"No thanks," I said in as normal a tone as I could. "I want to get really good at these small ones first."

"Excellent plan. Well, until our paths cross again, either on land or at sea, I bid you farewell."

"Bye."

I watched Hershel swim back to the crowd. As soon as I saw him riding another wave, I started to paddle back to shore. Now that I was alone, I was crying. Who was I fooling? I was no good at surfing. The only thing I was good at was snowboarding. I had no business being in the ocean. I belonged on a mountain. I belonged in Wyoming, not Los Angeles.

I had my back to the ocean, and I guess I was too wrapped up in how sad I was to realize that there was a surfer bearing down on me. The next thing I knew, someone crashed into me. I felt something hit me hard in the shoulder. I fell off my board and somersaulted underwater. I swallowed a whole bunch of water before I could get back to the surface. I coughed when my head came up. I tried to stand, but the water was too deep. And it was hard to swim because my leg was tangled on something.

"Grab this." I heard a voice say. My surfboard was now in front of me, so I grabbed it. "Are you okay?" the voice asked.

I turned around, and there he was—the boy with the blue eyes. "Uhh, yeah," was all I could manage to get out.

"I yelled, but I guess you didn't hear me," he said.

"Sorry," I said. "Are you okay?"

"I'm fine," he said, smiling. "I've had much bigger wipeouts than that."

"I'm sorry for being in your way."

"No worries," he said and smiled again. He had such a nice smile. I was too embarrassed to smile back. I really wanted to disappear. He laughed.

"It looks like are leashes are tangled up."

In a flash, Pam the Lifeguard swam up to us with a red floating thing and everything. "Is anyone hurt?" she asked firmly.

"No," he told her.

"And I'm fine."

"I don't want to take any chances. Whenever there's a collision, there's always the possibility of a concussion. Here," Pam got on back of the green giant. She motioned for the boy with the blue eyes and me to get on, "I want to check you both out on shore." Pam paddled us back to shore while the surfing class stared. I wanted to disappear.

Pam made sure that we weren't hurt, and then the boy with the blue eyes went back out. I was definitely done for the day. I waited on the shore for the rest of the class to finish. I was beyond embarrassed. How could I have done something so stupid? I sat on the sand and stared down the shore. I started daydreaming about snowboarding. I couldn't tell if it made me feel better or worse.

"You stay away from him." Suddenly, I was brought back to reality. Portia was standing above me, her hands on the hips of her designer wetsuit.

"What are you talking about?" I asked.

"Don't play stupid, Wyoming. Jake is mine."

"What are you talking about?" I asked again. "Who's Jake?"

"Boy, you really are dumb. Everyone knows who Jake is. He's only the hottest boy in school. And. . ." Portia leaned into me, "he's my boyfriend."

Jake is the boy with the blue eyes—and he's Portia's boyfriend. Perfect.

"I'll stay away from him," I said, staring down at the sand. It wouldn't be a problem avoiding Jake, because I decided I was never going to surf again.

# CHAPTER TWELVE

## LOST

When I got home from the disastrous surfing experiment, I ran straight to my room and shut the door. Still wearing my damp bathing suit, I sat down on the foot of my bed and called Sally. We talked for a few minutes and I felt a little bit better about things. I told her that I wasn't a good surfer. I told her about Portia, that Portia was pure evil. I told her about Jake and his blue eyes, and about Hershel, too. She listened to everything, then told me that it was going to take me a few more days before I became the most popular girl in school *and* a professional surfer. I laughed. Sally always had a way of making me feel better.

About twenty minutes into our conversation, she had to get off the phone. I still wasn't used to the time change from Wyoming to the West Coast, so her cutting our conversation short really caught me off guard. It was two hours earlier in California, so it was already ten o'clock back in Rockville. Sally's parents were very strict about her not talking on the phone past ten.

After I hung up with Sally, I walked down the hall to find my dad. I needed to talk. I found him in the living room, sound asleep on the couch. I was bored and lonely, so I picked up the phone again and made the call I had been avoiding for weeks—the call to Mom. Since we moved to LA, every time she called the house, I barely spoke to her. I mean, I was mad at Dad for taking me out here, but I was twice as mad at Mom for staying behind. Didn't she love me? Didn't she love Dad? Was her job *that* important?

She answered the phone on the first ring and sounded really excited to hear from me. We talked for a few minutes about what she had been doing the past few weeks. I told her a little bit about Los Angeles and my new school. For some reason, though, I put a positive spin on my life in California. I simply couldn't tell her the truth—that things had been going badly.

I *wanted* to tell her all about my failed attempt at becoming a surfer. I *wanted* to cry to her about the mean kids at David Hasselhoff. Instead, we talked about the Los Angeles weather and the beautiful pool in our backyard that Oscar liked to swim in. I told her about the Hollywood sign that I saw in the hills, the ocean, and the fact that every single day was sunnier than the last.

I was making small talk with my own mother. It was weird. But I just didn't want her to know how unhappy I was in Los Angeles. I thought that if I could make it seem great out here, maybe she would want to come out and join us sooner. I left a lot unsaid. And when I got off the phone with Mom, I had a strange feeling that she had left a lot unsaid as well.

After I hung up, I took a long shower to get the salt water off my body and to clear my mind. Then I got into bed early, trying hard to forget the disappointing day I had in the water. My bathing suit, which hung on the back of my door to dry, was an annoying reminder of the day's failure. I could still smell the salt water on it. Oscar noticed me looking at the suit, so he stared over at it too. Then he barked a small bark.

"I don't get it either, boy. How could I have been so bad?" Oscar sat at the foot of my bed. He cocked his head the way he always did when I talked to him. "I mean, I was horrible." I jumped up out of bed and paced around my room. Oscar followed behind me. Even with all of my stuff unpacked, my room still seemed empty. I felt empty as well.

I walked up to my bookcase. On the top shelf, I had arranged my favorite snowboarding awards. I didn't bring all of them with me to Los Angeles, just the important ones. I looked up at the awards. They gleamed in the sunlight that came in through the window.

The most important trophy—the one that really meant a lot to me—read: Mount Blizzard Snowboarding Championship, Second Place, Cece Morgan

It's the only second-place medal I ever kept. That's because the Mount Blizzard Snowboarding Championship is one of the biggest snowboarding competitions in Wyoming. Just to compete in it, you have to win at least four other local events—so everyone you're up against is really good. Last year was the first year I was old enough to qualify, and I did awesomely well.

I have a Mount Blizzard trophy at home for first place in my age group, but I'm more proud of the second-place award. In my first year of competing, I was second among the best snowboarders in the state. I reached up and grabbed the Mount

Blizzard trophy, a two-level type, with a sculpted snowboarder on top. It was heavy and felt cool against my skin.

I remember standing there during the awards ceremony. I was so happy. The guy who won was sixteen years old, the oldest you could be and still compete at Mount Blizzard. I remember that as they handed the winner's trophy to him, I hoped that the next year I would win. That, of course, was before I found out that I would be moving to southern California, and wouldn't even be there to compete at Mount Blizzard. I let out a loud sigh and put the trophy back on the shelf. Then I crawled into bed and fell asleep.

I had the strangest dream that night. I was back in Rockville. It had just dumped about two feet of fresh powder. I was on the chairlift riding over one of my favorite runs, Bandits' Getaway. It was still snowing heavily, but it was sunny. I remember thinking that was strange. Beautiful, though. The snowflakes reflected little rainbows as they fell down to the ground.

I got off at the top of the lift, then sat down in the snow to attach my binding. That's when I noticed that there wasn't any binding. There wasn't even a snowboard. I was on a surfboard. Not a big surfboard like the green giant, but a smaller one like the one Mrs. Blossom rode.

I looked down at the board. There was an orange and green painting of a girl surfing. She was inside a giant wave and had an equally giant smile on her face. Her left hand touched the wave. The next thing I knew, I was flying down Bandits' Getaway. I made long, beautiful turns in the powder. Effortlessly and silently, I made my way down the run. I was at home on the mountain, but I was on a surfboard.

I looked down at the board again. The orange girl was still

smiling in the giant wave. Suddenly, I realized that this shouldn't be happening. I should not be surfing down a mountain! I could not be surfing down a mountain! This was all wrong! And that's when I lost it. Suddenly the surfboard came to a dead stop in the snow. I flew off. Because I was moving so fast, I launched pretty high. I could see the rest of the run from the air. I was about to do a huge face-plant when I woke up.

After a dream like that, I figured I *needed* to go snowboarding. At breakfast, I told my dad that I wanted to try out Big Bison this weekend.

"Chili, that's three hours away."

"Well, we better leave early then," I said, with determination in my voice.

Dad put down his coffee and looked like he was going to say something. I could tell that he wanted to try and talk me out of it. The last thing he wanted to do on his day off was drive six hours round trip to Big Bison. When he looked into my eyes, though, he could tell this was not a fight he was going to win. I was going snowboarding this weekend. He was driving. I was owed at least that much.

"Sounds like a plan," he said, accepting his fate.

I woke him up at five on Saturday morning. "Come on, Dad, it's time to go." I said shaking him. He slowly opened his eyes. Then I turned on his radio full blast. His eyes opened wide and he jumped out of bed. "Well, I'm up now. Thank you, Chili," he mumbled sarcastically. "You sure you want to do this today?" he asked after a huge yawn.

"Of course I'm sure. I want to get there right when it opens."

Twenty minutes later, we were loading up the car. It felt

great to unpack my snowboard and all my gear. Oscar wanted to come, but we had to leave him home. "We'll be back soon, boy," I said, scratching his ears. Oscar gave me a look that told me he was sad and mad at me.

The ride up felt like it took forever. My dad had to stop to go to the bathroom three times because he was drinking so much coffee. Most of the time we didn't talk. I didn't have much to say. I didn't like school, I wasn't good at surfing, I sort of had one friend. It was all stuff I didn't feel like talking about anymore.

My dad's show was doing really well. He was having a great time and everyone seemed to like what he was doing. That was good news—but I didn't really want to talk about that either. I guess in the back of my head I was hoping his show would tank and we would have to move back to Wyoming. That scenario was looking less and less likely.

We'd been in Los Angeles for nearly three weeks now, and my mom still hadn't come out. Every week, an unexpected trip came up or she had to work on a project over the weekend. There was always something. I definitely didn't want to talk about that.

So, instead of talking, I looked out the window most of the time. It took about two hours to get into the less populated areas. We'd pass a small town, and then there'd be wilderness. I started to feel at home. I wondered when we were going to start seeing snow. We kept on driving, and there kept not being any snow. Finally, the road started to get steep and curvy, which I thought was a good sign. After a while of this, though, I still didn't see any snow. I was starting to get worried. How could there be a ski resort if there wasn't any snow?

We eventually came to a sign that read: Big Bison—Next

Right. And a moment later, we pulled into a huge gravel parking lot. The mountain didn't open for another half-hour, but the parking lot was already pretty full. I looked up and saw a white mountain in front of me, though there were spots on the mountain that weren't white.

I couldn't understand how there was snow on the mountain but none in the parking lot. We opened the car doors, stepped out, and walked up to the ticket booth. As my dad was buying my lift ticket—which, by the way, was more than twice as expensive as a lift ticket in Rockville—I asked the cashier how there was all the snow on the mountain.

"Snowmakers," said the cashier, without looking at me.

"Excuse me?" I asked.

"We've got the most sophisticated snow-making machines in all of southern California. Some people say it's better than real snow."

I soon realized that the people who said that the fake snow was better than real snow were idiots. This stuff was not better than real snow, or even half as good as real snow. By the time I had taken my first run down the mountain, I was pretty disappointed. Sure, it was awesome just to be snowboarding again. And, yes, driving three hours to kinda snowboard was better than not snowboarding at all. But still, this wasn't the same sport I had grown to love back home.

I got off the chairlift after my first run and stood on my board daydreaming. Snowboarding is the best sport in the world, even under these conditions, I thought. Then, for some reason, another thought popped into my head: surfing is probably the second best sport, even though I suck at it. Where did that come from?

Did I really like surfing? I rolled this last thought around for a moment. Yeah, I guess I did like it. I just wasn't any good at it. Too bad, because though southern California is a great place to surf, it didn't seem such a great place to snowboard. I shook these strange thoughts from my head and got ready for my next run.

I slid over to a spot where I could put on my binding. It felt great to just be on my board again. And it was nice knowing that, though the snowboarding here was far inferior to snowboarding back home, when I needed a quick fix, I could get one at Big Bison. I strapped into my board and headed down the mountain for my second run.

The first fifty yards or so was okay. I started to pick up some speed, but it was tough. I had to navigate in between several other less experienced snowboarders. What was worse, the surface was awful. My board didn't move the way it did back home. I can't really explain it, except to say that the fake snow was stickier than Rockville snow—the stuff that I was used to. It held on to my board and made my turns feel sluggish and my run feel slower.

Everything looked strange, too. No giant pine trees covered in snow or white mountain tops with clouds above them. In their place were inexperienced snowboarders and a bunch of giant, ugly, snowmakers pumping out the "best fake snow in southern California." Ugh! I headed closer to them, though, in search of better snow, and a more fully covered surface.

Unfortunately, the snow wasn't any better by the machines. It was a little deeper, yes, but it was still too sticky. Plus, the machine spat out chunks of ice every so often and I was scared for my life. So I moved back to the middle, where all the skiers and snowboarders were. A minute later, I finished that run and went back on the chairlift for another.

My next run felt pretty good—at first. For a moment, I even forgot where I was. I forgot about the lines and the people everywhere, too. I pretended I was back home in Rockville and it worked for a bit. Eventually, though, about halfway down, it stopped working. I realized exactly where I was. That pretty much killed my moment.

I had been at Big Bison for about forty minutes now and I was starting to notice that the mountain was really filling up. I couldn't believe how many people had arrived since I had. As I took my next run, I realized that the snow was getting too packed to the ground by the many snowboarders. In the spots where the most people were skiing and snowboarding, it had turned brown from mixing with the dirt. Long grass and twigs sticking up in a few places, too. It looked awful, sort of depressing. Very depressing.

People were falling in front of me and turning right into me every few seconds. I felt like I was in an obstacle course, but not a fun one. Twice, my board scraped over the top of a rock that I couldn't see poking out of the ground. I pictured the huge, ugly, scratch it must have made.

When I got to the bottom of my fourth run down the so-called mountain, I pulled off my goggles. I was finished. Not only did that last run scratch my board, but it was probably the worst run I'd ever had in my life. When I looked back up the mountain, I noticed that the line for the chairlift was even longer than before. Yup, I was done with Big Bison.

I found my dad in the lodge reading a book. "I'm ready to go home now," I told him.

He looked surprised to see me. "But we just got here an

hour ago."

"Well, I'm not snowboarding anymore," I told him. I don't really know why, but my lip started trembling and I nearly started to cry—again.

"Hey, it's okay, Chili, we can go home." My dad reached out and touched me on the shoulder. "What happened?" he asked.

"Nothing, it's just not like snowboarding at home. Three-hour drive, long lines, lousy snow—it started out all right, but then the mountain got crowded, it was muddy, I just think . . . " I paused, not sure what I really wanted to say. "It's just too frustrating, Dad. It makes me miss home too much." I took a deep breath. "Thanks for trying. This place just doesn't make me feel good." I spoke sadly.

When we loaded up my snowboard on top of the car, I saw two big scratches from the rocks. I was quiet all the way home.

# CHAPTER THIRTEEN

## BAD TO WORSE

On the Monday after my visit to Big Bison, school was not much fun. I was hoping that snowboarding would rejuvenate me, but it did the opposite. It seemed as if all of the energy had been sucked out of me. Snowboarding in California was not like snowboarding in Wyoming. I was an athlete without a sport.

The fact that Big Bison was a big disaster was one thing. When I coupled that with the surfing situation—the only other sport I actually liked—my life seemed hopeless. I couldn't snowboard because the conditions were terrible, and I couldn't surf because *I* was terrible.

Mrs. Blossom was alone when I walked into her first period class. "Hey, Cece." She didn't waste any time before asking, "Are we going to see you at Surf Club on Wednesday?"

I could feel my heart beating through my chest. "Oh, I don't know if I can make it on Friday. There's a lot of stuff that my dad and I have to take care of. You know." I had no idea what I was talking about.

I'm pretty positive that Mrs. Blossom could tell that my dad and I didn't have anything important to take care of. She leaned in close to me. "Can I tell you a secret?"

"Sure."

"I used to be one of the worst surfers ever."

"You?" I asked. I couldn't picture Mrs. Blossom being bad at anything, especially not surfing. It seemed like she was born to surf.

"Oh, I was a joke in the water. It took me three months before I stood up for the first time. And that was with surfing every day!"

"Wow." That's a long time to be horrible at something. "Why did you keep doing it?" I asked.

"I loved being in the water. It didn't matter to me that I wasn't getting better. I was just happy to be in the ocean."

I could kind of see what she was saying, but I still didn't really understand the point of doing something that you're not good at. I had never understood that, even in Rockville.

"Is there any chance we'll see you after you and your dad take care of things? Mrs. Blossom winked at me.

She had me cornered. "We'll see," I said. "Things really have been busy with us getting settled in the house." I didn't know what else to say. Although I knew that deep down I liked the sport of surfing, I really didn't want to embarrass myself again.

Hershel walked in and saved me. "Excellent morning to you, Cece—and excellent morning to you, Mrs. Blossom." I smiled at the sight of my only friend in Los Angeles.

"Morning, Hershel," said Mrs. Blossom.

The class began to fill up, and Mrs. Blossom moved to the front of the room. "Take your seats, please—we've got a lot to cover today."

We sat down. I hadn't realized it, but Portia was already there. She looked at me from across the room and her eyes shot imaginary daggers at me. Oh, how I dreaded and disliked her.

In the middle of Mrs. Blossom's lesson, I felt a tap on my shoulder. I turned around. A boy behind me, whose name I didn't know, handed me a note, folded into a neat rectangle. The outside was marked in red ink: For stupid Cece. I opened up the note and in the same red pen, it read: Stay away from Jake, stupid!

It didn't take a genius to figure out that the note was from Portia. Who else would be that mean? I looked over at her and she glared back, shooting more daggers my way.

I tried to ignore her for the rest of class. The bell rang. I waited for Portia to leave before I did. Hershel was nice enough to wait with me.

When we got to the hallway, Portia was standing next to Jake. She was acting all nice and sweet to him. I didn't get it. Jake seemed like such a good guy. Didn't he see how horrid Portia was? Didn't he care how mean she was? Portia noticed me staring at her and flashed me an evil grin. Then she put her arm around Jake. He smiled. Portia kept smiling with her hideous grin. Couldn't *something* go my way, just once? I wondered.

How come when bad stuff happens, I mean really bad stuff, it always happens all at once? I'd already had a miserable week going when my dad picked me up after school that day. I was horrible at surfing, snowboarding in California was terrible, and the boy I liked was dating the girl I hated. That should have been enough bad stuff for a while, right? Well, all of that combined wasn't as bad as what my dad told me on the car ride home from school.

"Hey, Cece," he said flatly. "How was school?" *Uh, oh, he called me Cece.* Right away, I knew something was definitely wrong. The only time my dad ever called me Cece was when something was wrong or when I was in trouble. Dad tried to smile, but I could tell he was faking it.

"What's wrong?" Utter panic gnawed at my stomach.

"Umm, well, I don't really know how to say this, Cece." Dad fidgeted a bit in the driver's seat. I leaned up. "I was going to wait until we got home." He looked into my eyes. "Your mother called this morning."

"Okay," I was waiting for the bomb to drop. "So what?"

Dad swallowed hard. "Well, she thinks it might be best that she stays in Wyoming for a while."

"What do you mean, a while?" I asked. "Like a month or two?" This did not sound good.

"I'm not really sure, Cece."

"Are you guys getting a divorce or something?" I asked, yes, but I was fairly certain—at least I hoped—that I was being ridiculous, jumping to conclusions. My parents couldn't get divorced. They loved each other. Didn't they?

Dad paused for a moment. He looked . . . like he was in pain. "I don't know," he said, almost whispering.

"What do you mean you don't know?" I screamed. "How could you not know?" This vague, yet terrible scenario, made my stomach feel like someone had kicked me in it.

"Your mother can't leave her job right now and she's not thrilled about moving to Los Angeles."

Now I couldn't hold back my tears. They started pouring out. "Well, neither was I, but I still had to come out here!"

My dad pulled over to the side of the road. "Honey, I'm sorry," he said. He reached over to give me a hug. "Everything is going to work out. We just . . ."

"Don't touch me!" I screamed at him. "How can you guys do this to me? I hate you both!"

Dad tried to calm me down. "Come on, Chili, what do you say we go get some ice cream over at . . ."

I cut him off. "Don't talk to me! Just take me home!" I yelled, before putting my head in my hands and sobbing. Neither of us spoke the rest of the way home. But it wasn't home. It was just the place we lived.

The moment we got there, I grabbed Oscar and went up to my room. My giant room felt even emptier than before. I immediately buried my face in my pillow, so I barely heard Dad tapping at my door a few minutes later. "Can I come in, Cece?"

I didn't feel like answering. I didn't feel like moving.

A few seconds later, I felt him sit down on my bed. "Cece, can you please pick up your head? We need to talk."

"No." My voice was muffled coming through the pillow. When I opened my mouth, I could taste the fabric softener. It was bitter, but I didn't care. I didn't care about anything anymore.

"Can you please look at me?" Even through the pillow, I could hear the sadness in my dad's voice. Still, I wasn't moving. "Well, just listen then, I guess." It was quiet for a few seconds. "Neither your mom nor I are happy about this. . . ."

Then why are you doing it, I wondered.

"The fact is, though, we've been having some problems for

a while now, some things that we just couldn't work out." He paused for a second. "We need to spend some time apart. This would have happened even if we were still in Wyoming."

Yeah, right, I thought.

"I want to be honest with you as best I can, Cece. And honestly, I don't know what's going to happen. I don't know if we're going to get back together." He paused again. Even through the pillow I could hear him sniffle. Was he crying? "This may be permanent. I just don't know. We don't know. But one thing that will always be true is that your mother and I love you very much. Our problems have, and never will have, anything to do with you. I'm so sorry, Cece."

I didn't move.

My dad sniffed again and coughed. "Is there anything you want to say? Anything at all?"

I still didn't move.

I felt his weight rise off my bed. "Well, whenever you want to talk, I'm here. Sometimes talking about stuff makes you feel better. I could sure use someone to talk to. I love you."

I wanted to reach out and hug him to make him feel better. I wanted to sit down and figure out where he and Mom went wrong. But I just couldn't. I was too upset.

# CHAPTER FOURTEEN

## WAKING UP

I have never walked in my sleep before. But if it's anything like I imagine it to be, for the next couple of weeks I felt like that was exactly what I was doing—sleepwalking. All this stuff was happening around me, but I just plodded along. Zombie Cece.

I couldn't feel anything. I wasn't happy or sad or even hungry. I wasn't anything. School, Portia, my Dad, my mom, surfing, Jake, Hershel, and even poor Oscar—none of it affected me at all. I would be right next to something, and I felt like I was thousands of miles away.

My dad kept trying to talk to me, but I wasn't even listening to him. I mean, the thought "my parents are going to get divorced" was definitely in my head. It just didn't connect to anything. It bounced around my head like a pinball. I couldn't make it mean anything. That's weird, right? I didn't understand what was going on.

On the one-month anniversary of my time in Los Angeles, I

woke up to Oscar licking my face. I petted him and looked at the clock. 5:14. In the morning. The past few weeks had been absolute misery. I barely spoke to anyone—not even Sally, who was leaving me about three messages a day at this point.

"Come on, Oscar, it's not time to get up yet." I tried to make him lie down and go back to sleep, but he wasn't having any of it. He was wide awake. "Do you need to go out?" I asked.

Oscar thumped his little tail, smiled, and barked twice, which means yes. He then spun around in circles, just like he always did when he got excited. "Okay, okay!. Shhhh." I stretched and rubbed my eyes. Then I climbed out of bed and groggily made my way downstairs. The house was quiet. I opened the door for Oscar to go outside, but he just stood there next to me. "What's the matter, boy?" I asked.

Oscar looked up at me, looked outside, then back at me again. He didn't move.

"Come on, go outside," I said, motioning to the open door. Oscar sat down. What was wrong with him? "Don't you want to go out?" I asked. He looked up again, cocking his head and smiling. I didn't get it. As I took a step towards the door to close it, Oscar barked.

"What?" I asked him.

Oscar kept smiling and wagged his tail. He sure was acting weird this morning.

I opened the door again, but this time I stepped outside. A flash of gray poodle shot out in front of me. Suddenly, Oscar was running around the yard like a crazy dog, jumping over bushes and rolling around on the grass. I laughed for the first time in a while.

Oscar came up to me with his tongue hanging out of his

mouth. I looked down at him, and then up at the sky. It was mostly dark, but there was a hint of pink on the horizon. The patio was slightly damp and felt cool on my feet. Everything was quiet. At five in the morning, it was hard to tell Los Angeles was a gigantic, crowded, horrible city. It was actually pretty nice.

Suddenly, Oscar stood up and ran towards the pool. He barked at me to follow him, so I did. We stood at the edge of the pool. In the light of the early morning, the water looked thicker than normal. The pool made gentle lapping noises as the ripples washed over the side. Without warning, there was a big splash as Oscar jumped into the pool. I laughed, "Oscar, what are you doing, boy?"

He paddled around like he was in heaven. It was news to him that he couldn't go swimming this early in the morning. He was having a great time. Oscar swam up to where I was standing. He barked, asking me to come in. It did look like fun in there, but it was so early. Oscar barked again.

"Okay, okay," I said. "You know, you really are a crazy dog. Wait a second." I ran into the house and up the stairs, quickly throwing on my bathing suit. I ran back downstairs and jumped in the pool. The water was perfect. The moment I hit that water something changed inside of me. I felt awake for the first time in weeks. Oscar swam up to me. I pet his soggy head. "Thanks, Oscar," I said. He barked and we played in the water some more. I swam a few laps, deep in thought the entire time.

"What are you doing?" My dad was standing on the patio wearing his shaggy white robe and looking confused.

"Just taking a swim," I said.

"Oh," said my dad. He looked at Oscar and me in the pool. We were both smiling. "Can I come in?"

"Sure."

The next thing I knew Dad had jumped into the water. The three of us swam around for the next thirty minutes. It was probably the most fun I'd had since we moved to California. I thought about the people I knew back home in Rockville. I thought about how a lot of them would be pretty excited to be in a swimming pool with their dad and their dog at five o'clock in the morning. Life was funny like that sometimes. When you least expected it, something could happen that totally changed your perspective on things.

Heading to school that day, I felt like something inside of me had been knocked back into place. I had finally accepted my fate: I was in Los Angeles indefinitely, for better or for worse. There was no reason to fight it anymore. My parents weren't living together. They might even get divorced. Sally was a thousand miles away. Big Bison was a disaster area. Jake was dating Portia. There was nothing I could do to change any of these things. In the car on the way to school I decided that it was time I stopped letting things that I couldn't control make me sad. It was time that I took my life into my own hands. It was up to me to make myself happy again.

That morning, I went up to Mrs. Blossom's desk after class. She had a stack of papers in front of her and was marking one with a red pen. "Mrs. Blossom?"

She looked up at me. "Hi, Cece." She slid the paper to the side. "What's up?"

"If it's ok, I'd like to go out with the Surfing Club again."

Mrs. Blossom smiled. "Of course it's okay, Cece. You're always welcome. I'm so glad you're coming out again." She clapped her hands and gave me an excited hug. Mrs. Blossom was the best. "The waves are going to be great today," she predicted.

"Cool," I said. "Well, I'll see you later then." I headed out of the room.

"Cece?"

I turned around. "Yes?"

"It's fun to just be in the water."

I didn't exactly know how to respond. "Okay" was all I said.

# CHAPTER FIFTEEN

## STANDING UP

So, there I was with the green giant attached to my ankle. I stood at the shore watching the waves and the rest of the class riding them. I wasn't quite ready to go in yet. I was still recovering from the look Pam the Lifeguard gave me when she saw me arrive with the rest of the Surfing Club. It was not the most encouraging welcome back to the ocean.

Foamy water rushed up and met my feet. It was cold, but with the sun shining strong, it actually felt pretty good. I took a few steps into the ocean. Once I was up to my knees, I got on top of the green giant and began paddling. I paddled out to the side of the class, as far away from Jake and Portia as possible. I got to a spot where small waves were forming. I sat there, trying to see a pattern . If there was one, I couldn't see it yet.

I sat for a few minutes, gently bobbing up and down. I couldn't get over how hot it was out here. Especially since Sally had told me that it was still snowing back home! I smiled at the thought.

Just then, I noticed a wave approaching. I quickly turned around and started paddling as fast as I could. I dug my arms deep into the water like Hershel told me to do. Hershel had said he wanted to surf with me today, but I said no. It was nice of him to offer, but I just couldn't be this bad at something in front of anyone. It was hard enough for me to be back out in the ocean at all. I just had to do this alone.

As I dug my arms deeper, I could feel the board moving faster. I kept paddling. The wave approached. I kept paddling. Then I felt the wave pick me up. For a second or two, I was actually riding along with the wave. It was awesome! I was going so fast—I could really feel the power of the wave beneath me. My heart sped up in excitement. I kept paddling. Then, the wave passed underneath me and curled over without me inside of it. "That was close," I said to no one in particular.

I turned back around on the green giant and watched for more waves to come. I was determined now. I wanted the feeling I had just experienced to come again and again. A few more waves came through and I tried to ride each of them. It seemed like I was getting closer and closer to actually standing up on the green giant with every wave that came through. I was finally getting the feel of it.

I caught about five waves for a couple of seconds each, but never long enough to try and stand up on the board. Until the last one. This one actually crashed with me in it, and it was amazing. I flew on top of the wave faster than I had ever moved in the water. But when it was time to stand up, I was too scared—certain that if I stood up, I would crash and break my neck. So I just held onto the board tightly and rode the wave in.

I paddled back out past the break after that last ride. I was having so much fun, but I still desperately wanted another chance to stand up and ride one in. During the next few minutes, my spot was pretty calm. I was lying down on the board, taking in the sunshine and the sounds of the ocean. There were a few sailboats way out in the distance. I watched as they slowly moved across the horizon. The gentle splashing of the water over the front of the green giant was a soothing noise. I thought about what Mrs. Blossom said earlier. It's fun just to be out here. I smiled. She was right.

Then I froze. About twenty feet off to my right, I saw a pair of fins. Not like the flipper kind of fins a scuba diver wears, but the kind of fins that belong to an animal that could eat me—and there were two of them! I was too scared to do anything. I couldn't yell. I couldn't swim away. All I could do was watch in horror as the pair of fins moved closer to me. Nobody told me that there were really sharks in ocean!

I opened my mouth to yell, but only a dry, raspy sound came from my throat. I was about to be eaten by a pair of killer sharks, and no one would even hear me scream.

The sharks kept swimming closer. They were close enough to me that I could see water shooting out from their blowholes. Wait a minute, sharks don't have blowholes. Dolphins have blowholes. I looked closer at the pair of fins. Their shiny, almost metallic skin reflected brightly in the sun. One of the fins disappeared underwater for a second. Then it came up and water shot out from the top of its head.

I relaxed when I was certain that these were dolphins, not sharks. They swam up pretty close to me. Not close enough to touch or anything, but close enough to see their faces. They were awesome looking. As they sliced silently through the water, I could see their long, thin noses, giant foreheads, and their smiles. It really looked like they were smiling as they swam by. They had the same kind of grin Oscar wore when he was happy. Even though I was still a little freaked out, I smiled back at them.

I watched the dolphins swim away, until I couldn't see their fins any more. I felt really happy. I didn't even get upset when it was time to go home and I hadn't stood up on a single wave. I did get close, though. After that day in the ocean, I decided that if I had to live in Los Angeles, I was going to spend as much of my time as possible in the water.

The next day at school, Hershel came up to me in the cafeteria and sat down. He was acting even more excited than usual, which for Hershel is saying a lot. "Hello, my friend," he said. "I have excellent news."

"What's that?" I asked.

Hershel picked up his grilled cheese and avocado sandwich. He took at bite and chewed slowly. He swallowed and then took a sip of milk.

"Come on already, Hershel," I said, losing patience.

Hershel put down the carton and wiped off the milk moustache from his upper lip. "This is classified information, so don't go spreading this. I have heard from the source that Mrs. Blossom entered us in the Super Wave Junior Championships."

"What do you mean you heard from the source? Mrs. Blossom told you?" I asked.

Hershel nodded.

"How is it a secret if she told you?" I asked.

Hershel looked down at his plate for a second. "I like classified information." I suddenly realized that this piece of news was about as classified as the cafeteria menu.

"Can you tell me any more about the competition?" I asked. "Or is that a secret too?"

"I guess I can tell you," said Hershel. He leaned in closer and started talking in a hushed voice. "Mrs. Blossom said that the competition is to take place precisely one month from this coming Saturday. It's going to be held at Dolly Parton State Park. Eleven other schools will be competing." Hershel shifted his eyes back and forth to make sure that no one was listening. "That's all the information I can disclose at this time."

Besides thinking that Hershel would make a terrible secret agent some day, I thought about the tournament. I was sure my days of competing were over after I left Rockville for Los Angeles. But I really did like surfing—even though I had never actually surfed. I was sure that if I took a month to practice, though, I would get much better in a short time. I'd gotten so close yesterday.

Sure, I *was* probably a few years away from winning any competitions, but that wasn't going to stop me from entering them. I was lost in this thought when I was rudely interrupted. "Well, look what we have here, isn't this just the cutest pair of dorks you could ever hope to meet?"

There was only one person whose voice could sound so mean. I didn't have to look up to know that Portia. "What do you want?" I asked coldly. I lifted my head and saw Portia surrounded by a few of her clones.

"I heard that Mrs. Blossom entered us in a tournament," said Portia.

I looked at Hershel. "Some secret," I whispered.

Hershel flashed an embarrassed grin.

"We're here to make sure you don't do anything stupid," Portia continued, "like enter the competition. Everyone knows how bad you are, Cece. You can't embarrass David Hasselhoff Middle School. We have a reputation we don't want ruined by some small town loser."

Her little group of clones laughed and nodded. But something was different today. It had been since that morning in the pool. I had changed the way I thought about things. I was no longer going to sit back and let life happen to me—I was going to *make* things happen. Portia had made me sad. Now she was making me mad, really mad. And now I had the courage to do something about it. "Why do you spend so much of your time concerned with a dork like me? That's pretty lame." I stood up and faced Portia. "Don't you think you're pretty lame?"

"What did you just say to me?" she asked, a little angrily. She was clearly taken aback. I don't think very many people had spoken to her like this.

Hershel looked stunned by my aggressive response. He put his hand on my shoulder. "Maybe you should sit down and . . ."

"I got this, Hershel." I shoved his hand off my shoulder. Then I looked at Portia again. "You walk around like you own this school. You think you're like, the queen, or something. I've got some news for you, Portia, there are more of us losers than there are of you." A small crowd started to gather around us to see what was happening. "I think it's time that we start standing up for ourselves." Portia had opened something up inside of me, and once I started, I had to get it all out. A few people in the crowd cheered.

"You hear that?" I said. "We're not going to take it from you any-more. Do you know why?"

Portia looked different than I had ever seen her before. Her face was bright red and her mouth was turned kind of side-ways or something. If I didn't know any better, I would have said that she looked a little scared. "Why?" she asked.

"Because I know the truth about you." I said.

"Oh yeah, and what's that?" Portia asked.

"You're a scared little girl who hides behind her meanness. Take away all the mean things that you do to other people, and there really isn't anything else there." I moved even closer to her. "I know, Portia, that deep down, somewhere, you are jealous of us losers who *are* something. You get your clone friends to be horrible to us, but really you are all jealous."

"Me, jealous of you?" Portia laughed, but there was a ner-vous energy behind it.

"That's right," I said. Portia backed away from me a few steps. I continued. "I feel sorry for you. You might be the most popular girl in school, but I would never trade places with you. I like being something, even if it's a hick from Wyoming."

Portia let out a little gasp to respond, but nothing came out. There was more cheering and laughing from the growing crowd.

I kept talking. "So let me tell you what's going to happen from now on. You're going to leave me alone. I'm going to enter that surfing competition, and there's nothing you can do about it."

Portia was at a loss. One of her clones whispered some-thing in her ear. Then Portia started to speak, "Listen, Wyoming freak. . ."

"Shut up. I am not the freak and you will never call me that again. You got it?"

She didn't say anything.

I shouted at her. "I asked you a question! Do you understand?"

"Yes," she whispered.

"Good, then get out of my face and stay out of my way."

Portia looked like she was about to cry as she turned and walked away. I sat back down in my seat, my heart racing inside of my chest. I had never spoken to anyone that way before.

"Wow, Cece! That was stupendous, unbelievable, amazing—it was excellent!" said Hershel. "I had no idea you were so tough!" He grinned broadly. A moment later, though, it quickly turned more serious. "We've got some work to do, though, tough girl. We need to get you ready for the competition."

# CHAPTER SIXTEEN

## JUST DO IT

The next morning, I was nervous about school. I didn't know what Portia was going to do after I told her off. I was sure that she would regroup and think of the worst possible ways to be mean to me.

I didn't see her in the hallways before school, though I did see a few of her clones. They didn't say anything to me. I was sure that the first time I saw Portia I would know exactly how the rest of my school year was going to be. Either my bravery in the cafeteria would render her harmless or it would make her twice as committed to making me suffer. As I walked into Mrs. Blossom's first period English class, I knew I was about to learn which it was.

Mrs. Blossom began her lesson. As she was talking, I carefully glanced around the room. I saw Portia at her desk and expected her to jump out of her seat and attack me. When she noticed me looking at her, though, she avoided making eye contact and stared down at her feet. I kept staring at her—more out of confusion than anything else. She sat there slumped in her chair. She wasn't exactly frowning, but she looked a little like I felt after one of her attacks in the hall.

I didn't think it was possible for her to feel those feelings. I never thought of someone like her having feelings. But looking at her there, I knew that she definitely did. Even after all she put me through I felt sorry for her.

As the day wore on, and there was no confrontation, I began to feel more comfortable. People always say that the best way to deal with bullies is to stand up to them. I guess they're right. It looked as if Portia wouldn't be bothering me anymore. I felt like the weather as I walked to my next class—light and sunny.

That night, the phone rang while my dad and I were eating dinner. Dad was doing a lot of cooking these days. He was at the studio when I was at school, but he was home the rest of the time. And when he was home, it seemed like he was always in the kitchen cooking up something. Tonight we were having burritos. I have to hand it to my father—they were really good.

With the last bite of my burrito stuffed in my mouth, I got up from the table to answer the phone. "Hello," I said.

"Cece?"

"Sally!"

"I finally found you! Where have you been?" she asked.

"I've been hiding out." I sighed, "I've been pretty sad, so I'm sorry."

"I've called you like. . . "

"I know," I said, "can we forget it, Sally?"

"Sure." She paused. "You sound weird, Cece."

"Well, I'm eating a burrito, plus, I just fixed my entire life. It took some time, but everything is going to be fine now."

"I never knew anything wasn't going to be fine. Are you sure you're okay?"

"I am excellent, Sally." I said, stealing Hershel's favorite word.

"You sound like you've had one too many burritos."

I laughed. I was so excited to hear her voice. We had been e-mailing almost every day, but I hadn't talked to her in more than a week. I hadn't really been talking to anyone since I found out that my mom wasn't leaving Rockville.

"Can you talk?" she asked.

"Sure," I said, walking into our living room.

"Cool," said Sally. "Well, see, my mom ran into your mom the other day at Joe's Market." I knew where this was going. I hadn't told Sally about my parents splitting up. "They got to talking, and your mom told my mom that she's not moving to Los Angeles."

I didn't know exactly what to say. "That's true" was all I said.

"Why didn't you tell me?" asked Sally. I could hear a little bit of hurt in her voice.

"I don't know. I guess I didn't want it to be true. Once I tell you, then it's real, you know?"

"Oh," said Sally. "Well, do you want to tell me about it now?"

I still didn't feel like talking about it. I was getting by pretending that nothing was really wrong. It was still too new, too real, to talk about. I started getting a little choked up. "I don't think I'm ready yet, Sally."

She could tell I was getting upset. "That's okay, Cece, we don't have to talk about it. Whenever you want to, though, you know I'm here, right?"

"Yes," I said. I did know she was there, but it was still nice to hear. "Thank you."

"You don't have to thank me," said Sally. "That's what friends do." I smiled. "You know what else friends do?" she asked.

"What's that?"

"They come visit their friends in Los Angeles."

The little grin on my face turned into a full-blown smile. I screamed, "Are you kidding? When?"

"In a month! My mom talked to your dad and we both have break at the same time. I'm coming for a whole week! I already have my plane ticket and everything."

This was the best news ever! "We are going to have such a good time. I can't wait! Bring your bathing suit, because we have a pool," I said excitedly. I couldn't believe that Sally would actually be coming for a visit.

"I can't wait either," Sally said. "And, Cece, if you want to talk about anything before then, you can, okay?"

"Thanks, Sally," I said. I don't think there's a better friend in the world than Sally.

After I hung up, I realized Sally would be visiting during the Super Wave Junior Championships. Now I really needed to do well. Sally has only seen me win.

That night, before I went to sleep, I took out my Three Special Things from my nightstand drawer. I hadn't looked at them since I found out about Mom staying in Wyoming. I held the ceramic orange in my hand first, tracing my finger over the bumpy surface and looking closely at the glossy skin. The top layer was clear and clean. Underneath, though, the real orange skin looked old and shriveled. I had never noticed that before. Whenever I looked at the orange, I always thought it was perfect. It never occurred to me that the orange inside could be dried up.

I put on Mom's glasses next. The room turned fuzzy as I looked through the thick lenses. I looked over at my bookcase and the trophies on the top shelf. All of my awards looked like one big shiny blob. I smiled at Oscar. Even when he was out of focus, he still was a handsome dog. I turned my head and looked around my room. Through the thick lenses, it was hard to recognize everything—like the giant blob shaped like my dad that was moving toward me. I quickly took the glasses off. "What are you doing in here, Dad?"

"Your door was open," he said. "I just wanted to say goodnight." He walked over to my nightstand. "Where'd you get that?" he asked, holding up the picture of him and my mother on their wedding day. He took a long look at it.

"I've had it for a long time," I confessed. "Can you please put it down?" I could feel my face turning red. No one but Oscar knew about my Three Special Things. I wanted to keep it that way. My dad kept standing there, though. He kept starting at the picture frame. His eyes welled up with tears.

"Dad?"

"Yes, Chili?"

"Can you please get out of my room?" He was making me uncomfortable. He just kept looking at the picture.

"Sure, sweetheart," said my dad. He put the frame back on my nightstand and turned around to leave.

"Wait, Dad."

"Yeah, Chili."

"When you and Mom got married," I paused. "Did you ever think. . . "

He finished my sentence. "That we wouldn't stay married? Not a chance." He picked up the picture again and looked at it. "I thought we would be like this forever."

I swallowed hard so I could speak. I was finally ready to talk about this. "So what happened?"

My dad sat down on the foot of my bed. Oscar moved in closer and sat right on his lap. I sat next to him. "Your mother and I really loved each other a lot when we got married." He paused, "The truth is, Chili, she's the only woman I've ever loved."

I sighed. "It sounds like you're reading an anniversary card or something."

"Wait a second, it gets more interesting—and then it gets pretty sad." He sighed. "Well, eventually, your mom and I started getting really into working. We were both extremely motivated. We wanted to be successful. After the first couple years of being married, we began experiencing success in our jobs, which was great. But we also spent less and less time talking to each other—I mean really talking. I'm not sure if either one of us even noticed that it happened, Chili." Dad moved a few strands of hair away from my face and looked into my eyes. "Taking care of you and watching you grow up has been the only thing that's really kept us together. We both just love you so much—so we've been sticking it out. But during these past few years, it's gotten much worse. We've barely been speaking to each other." Dad's lower lip began to tremble, "Honestly, I never wanted to live apart from your mom, but this whole thing just kind of. . ."

I could tell that Dad was about to cry and I knew I wouldn't be able to handle that. So before he could continue talking I reached out and gave him a hug. "I just want you both to be happy. I don't want to make things harder on you guys. If you need to be apart, that's okay with me. I can handle it. You don't have to stick together just for me."

After I finished talking, Dad squeezed me so hard that I thought I was going to explode. "We're gonna be great. Everything is going to be great, Chili." He paused. I could hear him sniffling, too. "Just so you know—I will always love your mother. I mean, she's the reason you were born, and you're the greatest thing I have in life."

"Thanks, Dad." I smiled. "You're cool too." I held up my mom's glasses. "One last question: why does Mom have paint all over her glasses?" I handed them to him.

He held them in his hands and smiled. "Well, before she started working, she would paint almost every day. You don't remember that?"

"No."

"I guess you were just a baby. Well, you're lucky. She was absolutely horrible." My dad laughed.

"What kind of stuff did she paint?" I asked, smiling.

"She painted everything—landscapes, portraits, even some abstract stuff. The only thing her paintings had in common with one another is that they were awful. Paintings of dogs around the neighborhood came out having three legs and would be sort of greenish in color. In your mom's painting, a blue lake was brown." My dad laughed out loud. "She was probably the worst painter alive."

"Why did she paint so much then?" I asked.

"She loved it. It didn't matter to her that her paintings were ugly. She was the first person to admit that she wasn't any good. She'd finish a painting, and the paint would be everywhere—especially on her. Then she'd say, 'another disaster for the pile,' with a big smile. Then, she'd start another one." My dad looked at me and grinned. "That's your Mom for you. You remind me of her sometimes, Chili." He kissed me on the top of my head. "Anyway, goodnight."

"Goodnight."

Once Dad closed the door, I thought again about what Mrs. Blossom said—it's fun just to be in the ocean. Mom would probably enter the surfing competition no matter how bad she was at it. I looked at her glasses for a little while longer. I traced my finger over the specks of paint that covered the frame. Then I put my Three Special Things back in my drawer.

Without even thinking, I picked up the phone and called Mom. I knew it was late in Rockville, but I didn't care. She answered the phone on the third ring and we talked for over an hour. It felt so good to talk to her. I told her all about Los Angeles this time, not leaving out the important details. I told her that Dad had told me about her paintings. She laughed and promised to bring a few with her when she came out to visit Los Angeles. She said she still had a few she kept in the attic. We also talked about her and Dad. She said a lot of the same things he had.

I decided that I was going to have to let that be. I reminded myself not to get upset about things I couldn't control. If Mom and Dad didn't want to stay married, I wasn't going to get in the way. It was going to take some adjusting, though. I told Mom this and she started to cry. By the end of the conversation, Mom and I had a plan set for me to come home and visit Rockville for Christmas week. She promised to take the week off. We would shop in Jackson Hole, hang out with Sally, and I would be able to do all the snowboarding I could handle! I couldn't wait.

I said goodnight, turned off my light, and snuggled close to Oscar. When I closed my eyes, I realized that I felt happy. Sure, I was sad that my parents were probably not going to get back together. But I was happy because I knew in my heart that they both loved me, and whatever they ended up doing was going to make them happy. It was like a great weight had been lifted. Dad was right—sometimes it helps to talk about stuff.

# CHAPTER SEVENTEEN

## TRAINING

The next morning, I needed to talk to Hershel right away. I spotted him sitting under one of the giant palm trees in front of the school, staring at the tree, and writing notes on a pad of paper.

"Hey, Hershel, can I talk to you for a minute?"

"Absolutely, what can I do for you today?"

"Well, I've been thinking a lot about. . . " I couldn't finish my sentence. I just had to ask. "Wait, what are you recording?"

"I'm measuring the width of the base of this tree. I've been doing it every day since I moved here."

I was about to ask him why, but I knew that question would lead into a ten-minute lecture about the growth patterns of California palm trees. So I left it alone. "That's cool. Anyway," I said, "about this Super Wave Championship thing."

"Yes?" asked Hershel, grinning.

"Well, since I'm going to enter, I'd like to try and not totally embarrass myself."

"Excellent idea."

"Yeah, but, the thing is I'm a pretty bad surfer," I reminded him.

"You are an inexperienced surfer. That's all. It doesn't make you bad. I think you're excellent." What a surprise.

"Thank you, but I am pretty bad." I stared at Hershel's measuring tape, notepad, and pen. "Why do you think of all these funny things to do? Are you bored or something?"

He smiled. "Nope, not bored. The opposite of bored. I am so excited by everything that I just can't help doing whatever experiments come to mind. I don't care what people think about it. I like doing this stuff. So I just do it."

Hershel reminded me of what Dad said about Mom and her paintings. She just wanted to do it, so she did it. That's kind of how I felt about surfing. I mean, I definitely wanted to get better, but I was content to just do it because it felt right.

"Do you think that you can help me be a better surfer?" I looked back at Hershel. "Not that I need to be better—like—life-or-death, or anything. I just figure, if I'm going to do it anyway I might as well get good at it."

"I can definitely help you. If you'd like, we can start your training today." Hershel smiled. "Oh, this will be excellent—surfing is the best, second only to being on the moon."


Four hours later, we were back at Dolly Parton State Park. We suited up and I grabbed the green giant. As the class swam out towards the pretty sizeable waves that were forming, Hershel and I stayed back on the shore. "I am going to stand on a wave today," I spoke with determination in my voice.

"That's excellent, Cece. But before we start, let me tell you a little something about the waves you are going to be standing on." said Hershel.

"Umm, okay, but I want to get out there because. . . "

"An ocean wave is the most sacred thing on the planet." Hershel spoke in his storyteller voice.

"Interesting," I was not completely sure I agreed. In fact, I didn't get what was so amazing about a wave.

"Think about it, Cece. A wave is energy." Hershel held out his hand to the ocean. "Somewhere out there, the wind is blowing. The energy from the wind is transferred to the ocean—and a beautiful wave is born." Hershel put down his hand.

I smiled. "That's pretty cool, Hershel."

"The waves we're watching right now could have formed thousands of miles away. They could be washing up on the shore from a voyage that began near Japan."

I interrupted him. "My dad always talks about stuff like that. Like how a couple of kids our age might be in Japan right now, and one of them might be teaching the other one how to surf."

"That is most excellent." Hershel smiled again. It was hard not to catch some of his excitement. "Anyway, once you appreciate the waves, you start to realize that working *with* the waves is the only way to be a great surfer. You got me?"

I nodded my head. "With the waves. I got it." Then I grabbed my board and headed toward the ocean before Hershel started another story. Hershel left his board on the beach and chased after me. "Today is about you getting up on the board, Cece. I must have full mobility in our training," he said.

Once I reached the water, I dove onto my board. Hershel

swam alongside me past the breaking waves. I stopped paddling when the water was up above Hershel's shoulders. Then we waited on the ocean for a couple of minutes—me bobbing up and down on the green giant—Hershel in his superhero wetsuit, treading water beside me.

Finally, the ocean started getting choppy. "Do you see it?" Hershel asked.

"Yes," I said, noticing a wave forming in the distance.

"Then turn around," Hershel spoke forcefully. "Start paddling like crazy! If you wait too long to catch the wave train, you won't be able to climb on board."

I turned around and started paddling.

"Excellent," said Hershel. "Paddle, paddle, paddle. Dig those arms deep in the water." I looked over my shoulder and saw Hershel behind me. He had his hands on the board and was kicking along as I paddled. The wave was coming closer. I kept paddling. "Paddle, paddle, paddle," shouted Hershel behind me. "Your arms are shovels—excellent, arm-shaped shovels."

I felt the wave come up under me. I kept paddling and digging my arms as deep as I could. Hershel let go. The force of the water behind me felt different—sort of the way it had felt a week earlier when I was finally able to catch one. Only this time, the force behind the wave was twice as powerful. The green giant got caught in the wave and started to really move—without me paddling. I was in the wave!

"Now jump up!" shouted Hershel, from a distance.

This was the hard part, but I had to do it. So I pushed my arms down on the board and jumped up to my feet like I had practiced on the beach with Mrs. Blossom. I nearly fell over, but after I regained my balance I looked up and realized that I was riding the wave. I was really surfing!

"All the way up!" shouted Hershel.

I stood all the way up. "Woohoo!" I couldn't believe it. I was surfing! The wave was moving me towards the shore, and I stood there smiling on the green giant. "I'm surfing!" I cried as the wave made a swishing sound underneath the board. It was beautiful. It reminded me of the sound a snowboard makes in fresh powder. But at the same time, it felt totally different. I was completely weightless, like I was flying or something. I shifted my weight and turned the board a little to the left. Then I turned the board a little to the right. It wasn't responsive like a snowboard, but it definitely moved.

The main difference between the two sports seemed to be in the movement of the board. When snowboarding, I used the stable ground below me to push *against* to turn or pick up speed. In surfing, the ground below me was constantly moving and changing shape, so I had to react to *it*—moving *with* it, not against it. It was just like Hershel had said before we stepped into the ocean— working with the waves was the only way to be a great surfer. This meant that every ride on a surfboard was unique. I loved that about surfing.

The wave kept moving me closer to the shore. I didn't want to crash into the sand so I closed my eyes and jumped off the green giant. Cool water rushed over me. My feet touched the soft sandy bottom. I stood up, opened my eyes, and took a breath. I had just ridden my very first wave. Right after I finished that ride, I grabbed my board and raced back out to catch another one. I was officially hooked.

Hershel swam up to me on my way out to him. "Nice ride," he said.

"That was the coolest thing ever!" I flung myself at Hershel and gave him a big hug. I was so excited. I felt as if I had just won a race. Hershel and I stared at each other for a minute after I let go of him. He looked pretty cute wearing that oversized wetsuit of his. "Thanks, Hershel," I said, quickly turning my head away and looking toward the shore.

"For what?" asked Hershel.

"I couldn't have gotten up on that wave without you."

"You just needed a little push. The rest was all you."

"Still, thanks," I said.

"My pleasure," Hershel said. "You looked beautiful riding that wave." Now it was him looking away from me. "I mean, you and the wave together—excellent." I turned around and looked at another wave that was forming.

# CHAPTER EIGHTEEN

## SURFER

We rode like that for the rest of the afternoon. After about an hour, Hershel went and grabbed his board, surfing right next to me. I no longer needed his help to get onto a wave. I really had the feel down at this point. I quickly realized that surfing wasn't about trophies, or proving something to Portia either.

It was all about the ride.

Speaking of Portia, she pretty much left me alone in the weeks leading up to the Super Wave Championships. It was almost as if I had a Portia Pass. She and all her clones just ignored me. I ignored them. They never apologized for being horrible to me, but not having to deal with them was great nonetheless

I saw Jake in the halls and at surfing club. I was realizing more and more that he was kind of a jerk too. I saw him give some innocent fifth-grader a wedgie in the hallway outside of art class. All of his friends were laughing and the kid he was tormenting was crying. Jake started to remind me of Portia. Sure, I would still stare at him when he wasn't looking, but I wasn't excited about him anymore. I decided that he was just like my plastic orange. Really nice looking on the outside, but dried up and ugly on the inside.

Dad's show was doing great! The country really liked Mad Marty in the Morning. Mom and I were talking every day and she was planning a trip out to Los Angeles for Thanksgiving. I was excited, secretly hoping she and Dad would fall in love again. Oscar, of course, was the world's greatest dog. And our kitchen table was much nicer than the table back home. It didn't have those bizarre designs on it like the table in our Wyoming kitchen. It was simple with big white tiles on the top. So that was great too.

During the next few weeks, Hershel and I went surfing as much as we could. Sometimes we went with the Surf Club and sometimes it was just the two of us. He really helped me a lot. Every time we went out, I felt myself getting better and more comfortable in the ocean. I didn't need to use the green giant anymore either. The smaller boards were much harder to surf on, but every time I went out I improved.

Things were going very well until about a week before the event. Nothing changed, and nothing out of the ordinary happened. I just started getting nervous. Once I learned how to surf and started to make dramatic improvements, the competition started to mean more and more to me. The realization that I would be competing, and probably *not* winning started to set in.

I tried to explain this to Hershel before we went in the ocean. His response was totally Hershel. "What exactly is so important about winning?" He asked me this as he rubbed sticky wax on his board.

"What do you mean?" Asking why winning was important

was like asking why the sky was blue—it just was.

"Why do you feel like you have to win?" Hershel wasn't backing off.

"Isn't that why *you* compete?" I asked

"Not me." Hershel stared up at me from his board. "I surf for the ride. I compete for the heck of it. Don't think that means I'm not excited for the event. I love being around people who enjoy the same things I do. Plus, I plan on recruiting some new members to the Lunar Club. I've made new surfer-friendly pamphlets that I'll be handing out." He put down the sticky wax and turned serious. "Surfers need to appreciate the moon, Cece—there would be no tides without the moon. No tides, no waves—no waves, no surfing."

We paddled into the ocean. It was a beautiful day. The sunlight hit the tops of the waves and lit up a million tiny mirrors. I breathed in the clean salty air through my nose and smiled. The waves were much bigger than the ones we usually rode. I watched a big wave break ahead of us. As it loudly crashed down, I realized that my heart was beating fast.

"Looks like the ocean is a little more excited today." Hershel remarked.

I nodded.

"Do you want to head back to shore?"

The expression on my face must have given me away. On the mountains back home, there wasn't a run I couldn't handle. I was never scared when I was snowboarding—I always knew exactly what I was doing. But surfing made me feel kind of out of control.

Something made me not turn around, though. Maybe it was

that deep down I knew the only way I was going to get better was to try something I was uncomfortable with. Maybe it was Hershel's goofy grin and his giant blue wetsuit. If *he* could be out in the ocean, excited to take on big waves, then I could be too.

"No. Let's keep going."

"Excellent."

We had to paddle out past the breaking waves before we could catch them. This was a huge challenge because the waves were enormous and continued to break on top of us, pushing us backward as we tried to move forward. I closed my eyes and pushed the front of my board down with my hands like Mrs. Blossom had taught me. It was called duck diving, though I had no idea why a duck would ever dive into a big wave. The cool water rushed over me. I could hear the largeness of the wave as it passed. I popped back up and immediately started paddling. I made it past the breaking point and caught up to Hershel.

"Fantastic work, Cece."

I smiled at Hershel.

"Are you ready to take a ride?" he asked me.

"I think so." I was as ready as I was going to get, but these waves were huge!

"The next good wave is all yours."

We bobbed up and down as we scanned the ocean for a good wave. I spotted something forming in the distance. I turned around and paddled as hard as I could. I looked over my shoulder. "Don't look back!" Hershel yelled. "Just keep paddling!"

I dug my arms deeper into the water. My board started to pick up speed. I could hear the wave growing behind me. My heart was beating fast again, but this time out of excitement. My board rose up as the giant wave made its way to the shore. I could see the lip of the wave forming right in front of me. I could almost predict exactly how this monster would break. I dug as deep and hard as I could into the water. My board got caught in the wave perfectly— right at the top. As fast as I could, I pushed up into a crouch, my board still in the middle of wave.

The wave was moving really fast, and I was in it. I stood all the way up. I was flying. Once I was up, I knew exactly what to do. The control of the smaller board was a lot better than the green giant. It wasn't like a snowboard, but it moved pretty well. I shifted my weight and made small turns on the wave. I made a few wider turns. It was awesome. Even though I was in the ocean and it was seventy-five degrees out, I felt for a second like I was back at home.

I made a bigger turn towards the curl of the wave. The turn was a little too big, because the next thing I knew, I was caught in the lip of the wave. Then I was thrown backwards into the ocean. The water stung my back as I hit the deck. It didn't hurt too much, though. I'd been through worse. The wave crashed over me and I somersaulted a few times underwater, but I wasn't scared anymore. I knew that the wave would pass and then I would be able to come back up.

When I came up, Hershel was right next to me. "That was quite a wipeout. Are you okay?"

"I am most excellent." He laughed. I laughed. My grin was almost as big as the grin Hershel wore. I might not know exactly what I was doing out in the ocean, but it sure was a lot of fun.

# CHAPTER NINETEEN

## THE RIDE

The Super Wave Championship was on Sunday. Sally came into town on Saturday, the day before the event. My dad and I picked her up at the airport. It was so good to see her. We hugged for what seemed like forever, then headed home.

It was Sally's first time to California, and, to say the least, she was a little excited. "I can't believe you guys live here," she said, looking out the window into the sea of cars and never-ending concrete. "You guys are so lucky. This place is awesome!" She pointed to her right. "That whole street is bigger than Rockville. Wow. Look at the green hair on that guy. There's the Hollywood sign! It's huge!"

Sally was in heaven.

"When are we going to Disneyland?" she asked, bouncing up and down on her seat. She noticed a stylish woman walking down the street. "Was that a movie star? Should we stop and get her autograph?"

It was good to be with my friend again.

Sally was even more excited when she saw our house. "No way!" she said as we pulled into the driveway. "This is really where you guys live?"

I thought she was going to pass out when I showed her the pool. "If I lived here, I would spend every single second out here in the pool," she said. "I'd eat all my meals in the pool. I'd probably develop flippers I'd spend so much time in the water. Cece, this is absolutely amazing. I don't know how you ever didn't like it here. This place is the coolest place in the world—and I've only been here an hour."

We took a swim, and when we came out, I was almost as excited about the pool as Sally was. Sally was just like Hershel, she made you get excited about things.

We stayed up late that night talking and watching movies. We probably should have gone to bed earlier, but it was too good to be with Sally. I didn't want to waste a single minute. It was just like things were back home. We talked about everything, even my mother and father. I told her that my parents probably weren't go- ing to get back together and that I was okay with it. She gave me a hug and I cried a little, but I really was okay.

The next morning we had to get up really early. The cham- pionship started at seven. My dad woke us up at six. I was so tired. After we ate a small breakfast, we piled into the car and headed for Dolly Parton State Beach.

There was a small crowd already gathering when we got there. I spotted our club right away, but most of the kids I had never seen before. Mrs. Blossom was standing by the judges' booth. The butterflies were already performing in my stomach. This was the first time I would compete in anything since snowboarding in Rockville.

We spotted Hershel. He was hard to miss in his neon green shirt. As we got closer to him, I noticed that there was a homemade drawing of the moon on the front of his shirt and the words: The lunar club is out of this world. He wasn't kidding about trying to get new members. I introduced him to Sally. He turned to shake her hand and I noticed the printing on the back of Hershel's shirt: It might be roughly 238,855 miles away, but the moon is right next to my heart. Sally and Hershel talked for a few minutes while I went to fill out some forms and get my entry number.

When I came back, Sally was standing with Oscar and my dad. "Hershel seems really nice," she said.

"He is," I said. "He's like my best friend out here."

"He's strange, though, huh?" Sally asked. "I told him about how much I loved your pool—how I would spend all my time there if I lived out here, even during meals. He told me that he loved the water so much that he was working on inventing a waterproof pie so that you could eat a pie in a swimming pool or while surfing. He said he was also looking into waterproof mashed potatoes."

"Yeah, that's Hershel. He's great."

"Funny too," said Sally. "And I think he likes you."

"What makes you say that?"

"It's just a feeling I get." Sally shrugged her shoulders. "Could be nothing." Sally looked at all the other people on the beach. "Where's this Jake guy that you like?"

"I told you, I don't like him anymore. He has a girlfriend and she's a jerk. I think he's a jerk too."

"Point him out anyway."

I saw Jake in a crowd of boys from my class. He was talking with his hands like he always did. "He's that one over there ... in the orange and green shorts."

Sally looked at Jake. "Wow, he *is* cute. But I think Hershel's cuter."

"What are you talking about?" I asked.

"I think Hershel's cuter. I just do," said Sally.

I found Portia in the crowd and pointed her out to Sally as well. Sally made a circle with her left hand then clapped three times.

"What was that?" I asked.

"I just cursed her," said Sally. "I saw this thing on TV about witches. That's how they curse people."

"Thanks, I guess." I shook my head at her.

"No problem."

We hung around on the beach waiting for my turn to compete. There were worse places to be nervous. It was turning into a gorgeous day. Even at seven in the morning, the sun was shining, the air was clear, and it seemed like you could see down the shore all the way to Mexico.

The Super Wave Junior Championship was set up by boy and girl age groups. All the boys from all the schools in the same age group would compete against each other; then the girls in that age group would compete. The sixteen-year-olds went first. They were awesome. Some of rides were real killers. One girl did a 360, turning her whole board around on a wave. It was incredible.

"Can you do that?" Sally asked me.

"Not yet," I said. "A few weeks ago, I couldn't even get up on the board."

"Well, you could do that on a snowboard. I've seen it. I

bet you could surf circles around that girl."

I know that Sally was just trying to make me feel better. "Seriously, I'm still learning, Sally. Surfing and snowboarding are totally different," I said.

We watched more of the competition. Finally, it was the twelve-year-old boys' turn. We cheered Hershel on in his wetsuit that was still two sizes too big. Hershel was not the most graceful surfer in the world, but he was fearless. Any wave that was near him, he would take. He rode more waves than anyone else in the time he was out there. He was like a machine, and he did it all with a mile-wide grin on his face. I was yelling for Hershel louder than anyone else.

There was this kid from another school who was by far the best out there. This guy was amazing. He reminded me of Mrs. Blossom. It was like watching someone who was at home in the ocean, who was just doing what he was supposed to be doing.

I spotted Portia down the beach with a few of her clone friends. I noticed a few of them point to the amazing surfer and smile. Portia turned around and snapped something at them and they stopped pointing and smiling.

Sally looked at Portia and her friends. "You know what else about the Portia girl, her shirt looks like something my cat chewed up and spit out."

I laughed. I loved having Sally around.

When the boys' heat was over, it was my group's turn. Mrs. Blossom ran up to wish us all luck. She gave me a hug. "Good luck out there, Cece, and no matter what happens. . . "

"I know." She didn't need to finish her sentence. "I'm just going to enjoy the ocean."

There were about twenty girls or so in my age group. We were standing by the shore, waiting for the loudspeaker to tell us to start paddling. We had fifteen minutes in our heat. The judges scored our best two rides. A loud voice came from the judges' tent. "Twelve-year-old girls will start in five, four, three. . ."

I took a deep breath and jumped up and down on the sand.

". . .two, one, go!"

We took off paddling. A few girls were much faster than me and pulled out ahead. I noticed I wasn't the slowest one out there either, and that made me feel good. By the time I got to where the waves were breaking, a few girls were riding the first of them.

We were all spread out, hoping our positions would be where the next good wave would come. I spotted a nice one forming and quickly turned around and started to paddle as hard as I could. I just barely missed it. I felt it go under me as I watched a girl from another school catch a ride right next to me. "Okay, Cece, get the next one." I whispered.

I paddled back out again. I waited a little while, and pretty soon another wave was coming my way. I turned around and paddled hard, digging my arms deep. My arms started to burn, but I kept going. The wave came under me, and my board stayed with it. I paddled a few more strokes as the wave was about to curl over. I caught the wave and stood up on it. As soon as I was up on my feet, though, I lost my balance and fell over into the water.

The wave crashed over me, knocking me around under water. My board tugged on my leg as it was pulled to the shore. I came up to the surface and swam to my board.

"You got a little too excited there," I said to myself. "You can do this."

I looked up and saw Portia riding a wave. She definitely wasn't the best person out there, but she certainly wasn't horrible. I paddled back out.

"Ten minutes remain," shouted the man on the loudspeaker.

In the next five minutes, I caught two more waves. They weren't very long rides, but I stood up and was able to make a few turns on the board. I would say I somewhere right in the middle of the pack of girls—not the best, but certainly not the worst either.

"Five minutes remain."

I caught the next wave for my longest ride of the day so far. The problem was, it took me all the way to the shore. This meant that I had a long way to paddle back out. It also meant that I probably only had one ride left before time ran out. I paddled as fast and as hard as I could to get out past the break.

When I got there, I barely had a chance to catch my breath. A huge, beautiful wave was headed right towards me. I was in the perfect spot to catch the biggest wave I had ever seen in the ocean. I turned around as fast as I could, and started paddling. The only problem is that when I turned around, I noticed that Portia was right next to me. She was trying to catch the same perfect wave! We both paddled as the wave formed behind us.

"Get off my wave, Wyoming."

"No. It's my wave too."

The wave came closer as we paddled next to each other.

I dug my arms deeper. I pulled slightly ahead of Portia. I kept paddling as hard as I could. I was about half-a-board's length in front of her when the wave arrived. We both popped up at the same time. Only I was in the right spot. I stood all the way up, just as Portia wiped out behind me.

The wave was huge and I was going so fast that I was a little scared at first. That fear quickly turned into total excitement and a deep concentration. Everything seemed to disappear around me. It was like I was alone in the wave. For those few seconds, it was as if time slowed down to a stop. I could hear my surfboard's fin slicing through the water. I could feel the wave underneath my board. Every movement I made was in sync with the wave. We were one. I knew exactly what it was going to do and I rode *with* it, not against it. I had never felt more alive.

I carved beautiful Cs, just like my name. Cece was here. Cece was here.

For that one ride, I was the best surfer in the competition. I rode that wave like I had been surfing my entire life, not just a month. I stayed on longer than any ride I've ever taken. And when the wave peeked, about fifty yards from shore, I shot up and did an awesome carve—just like the sixteen-year-old surfer I had seen earlier in the competition. I slid up the wave, getting some air at the top, then landing perfectly in the wave. It was awesome. "Woohoo!" I shouted.

It was only when the wave reached the shore and I saw all the people on the beach applauding me that I remembered that I was at a competition. I jumped off my board. I knew I hadn't won, because that was my only epic ride, but I hadn't embarrassed myself either. I was definitely a legit surfer.

Oscar was pretty easy to spot in the crowd. He was the only standard poodle at the Super Wave Championship. Sally was holding his leash, cheering and jumping up and down like a crazy person. Hershel was standing next to Sally going nuts. My dad was going nuts too, only this time, he was dressed in shorts and a t-shirt.

He left his gorilla costume at home. My face hurt I was smiling so much.

I turned around and saw Portia swimming back to shore. "Guess it was my wave after all," I called to her.

I noticed Jake walking towards me. At first I thought he was coming to help Portia, but he came right up to me. "Wow, Cece. That was an incredible ride. You really nailed that carve. I had no idea you were so good." Jake said.

"Thanks." I just looked at him.

Jake stood there in front of me, smiling. "Can I help you bring in your board?"

If Jake had asked me that two months ago, I would have been the most excited girl on the planet. I looked over at Hershel standing with Sally and Oscar. Then I looked at Portia dragging herself out of the water. She looked like a drowned rat.

"No thanks. But it looks like Portia could use a little help."

I left Jake and walked over to meet my friends and my dad.

"Oh, Cece, I am so proud of you. You surfed so beautifully out there. You are really good!" Dad looked amazed.

"Thank you," I said, giving him a hug.

Sally squealed with delight and joined us, "You are awesome, girl!"

Oscar licked my hand.

When I let go of my father and Sally, I noticed that Hershel was standing right behind me. "Excellent riding, Cece," he said.

I turned around to face him. "I couldn't have done this without your help, you know." The sight of him standing there in his wetsuit with the sun shining on his smiling face made me realize that

Sally was right—Hershel was really cute. And I did something that I totally didn't expect. I gave him a kiss right on his lips, in front of everyone—even my Dad and Mrs. Blossom.

Hershel smiled at me. "Excellent indeed," he said.

# CHAPTER TWENTY

# NIGHT SWIMMING

That night, after Sally fell asleep, I quietly went up to the trophy shelf on my bookcase. Oscar came up to me, and I patted his head. In my hand, I held the ribbon from today. It read: Super Wave Championship—Twelve-Year-Old Girls—Fourth Place.

I walked over to my nightstand, and I opened my drawer with the Three Special Things. I placed the ribbon next to the picture of my parents. I was going to have to rename this stuff My Four Special Things.

Oscar put his paws on my feet and licked my right ankle.

"Hey, boy, go wake Sally up." I told him, picking him up and putting him on the bed. He walked over to Sally and started licking her face.

Five minutes later she was awake and we were both in our bathing suits. The three of us ran downstairs to take a late night swim. Even at midnight, it was fun just being in the water.

# TEST YOURSELF...ARE YOU A PROFESSIONAL READER?

### Chapter 1: Big Chill

What is the "Big Chill?" Why did Cece feel so comfortable at the top of the "Big Chill?"

What sight caused Cece to move off-line and wipe out during the last heat?

Who was inside the gorilla suit?

### ESSAY

In Chapter 1, we are introduced to Cece. We learn that she loves to snowboard and about her relationship with her father. Now, write an introduction about yourself. Include details about where you're from, your family, your hobbies...etc.).

### Chapter 2: Growing up Chili

Why didn't Cece want people outside of Rockville to read the article that featured Rockville Mountain?

Why do most kids think Cece is lucky that Mad Marty is her father?

Who are Cece's two best friends?

## ESSAY

In this chapter, Cece begins to talk about what profession she would eventually like to pursue. What are some goals of your own that you're aiming to achieve in the years ahead? Have you picked out a possible profession yet?

## Chapter 3: The Phone Call and
## Chapter 4: Cece and Sally

How did Cece feel about the possibility of moving to Los Angeles?

Where do Sally and Cece meet when they need to talk about important stuff?

What is Big Bison? What did Cece think about her snowboarding future after she called Big Bison?

## ESSAY

In these chapters, it becomes clear that Cece and her dad are going to move to Los Angeles. Have you ever moved before? If so, describe your feelings when you had to relocate. If you've never moved, what is one place where you'd like to move? Explain how moving might affect you.

## Chapter 5: The Rearview Mirror and
## Chapter 6: Entering Los Angeles

What are Cece's Three Special Things?

What was in Cece's 'Just in Case' box? Why did she call that box her 'Just in Case' box?

What was Sally's "going-away" present for Cece?

## ESSAY

Cece takes one last ride on Rockville Mountain before she leaves town. Again, her obvious love of snowboarding is displayed. Detail a sport or hobby that you enjoy. Why do you like this particular sport/hobby?

## Chapter 7: New School Disaster and Chapter 8: The Magician

Why did Cece immediately feel comfortable with Mrs. Blossom?

How did Cece know Hershel's name before he even said a word to her?

Who followed Cece into the girls' bathroom when she was upset? How did this person know exactly how Cece was feeling?

## ESSAY

From these chapters, we learn that Cece has a favorite teacher, Mrs. Blossom. Who is your favorite teacher or coach? Explain why this person is your favorite teacher or coach. What have you learned from him/her?

## Chapter 9: The Big Blue Ocean and
## Chapter 10: Surf's Up

Where did Cece's dad take her after she had a bad day at school?

What good news did Mrs. Blossom have for Cece when she saw her at the beach?

What does Hershel call robotic monkeys?

### ESSAY

Portia has become a pain in Cece's side with her constant harassment. Why do you think that Portia goes out of her way to make Cece feel unwelcome? Explain.

## Chapter 11: Collision Course and
## Chapter 12: Lost

Why was Hershel laughing when Cece told him that her foam board might be broken?

Why didn't Cece tell her mom the truth about her time in Los Angeles?

What did Cece think of the fake snow at Big Bison?

### ESSAY

In Chapter 12, Cece is disappointed with the snowboarding conditions at Big Bison. Write about a time in your life when you had high expectations, but ended up being disappointed. Or, write about a time when someone or something exceeded your expectations.

### Chapter 13: Bad to Worse and
### Chapter 14: Waking Up

Why was Cece paranoid when her dad called her "Cece" instead of "Chili?"

Why did Cece feel like she was "sleepwalking" through life?

When does Cece "wake up" in Chapter 14?

### ESSAY

Cece has had some unfortunate occurrences in her life up to this point. Yet, in Chapter 14, she "decided to stop letting things that I couldn't control make me sad." What does she mean by this? How could you use Cece's words in your life?

### Chapter 15: Standing Up and
### Chapter 16: Just Do It

What animal did Cece actually see when she thought that sharks were swimming around her?

What good news did Hershel share with Cece during lunch?

What does Cece discover about the best way to deal with bullies?

In Chapter 15, Cece overcomes a fear of hers by "standing up" and confronting Portia. How did Portia react to Cece's tough response? Detail an instance in your life when you had to deal with a bully or simply overcome a fear.

## Chapter 17: Training and
## Chapter 18: Surfer

According to Hershel, why is he always busy with various experiments?

When did Cece become "officially hooked" to the sport of surfing?

What did Cece eventually realize about Jake?

**ESSAY**

In these chapters, the fact that Hershel believes in Cece and her abilities is obvious. In turn, Cece begins to believe in herself. Why is it so important to believe in yourself? Do you believe in yourself? Explain.

## Chapter 19: The Ride and
## Chapter 20: Night Swimming

What did Sally think about Cece's home in Los Angeles?

How did Sally "curse" Portia? How did Sally learn this technique?

What item became Cece's Fourth Special Thing?

## ESSAY

Congratulations! You have completed another Scobre Press book! After joining Cece on her journey, detail what you learned from her life and experiences. How are you going to use Cece's story to help you achieve your dreams? What did Cece teach you about trying new activities that you aren't necessarily skilled in?